The Riding School Connemara Pony

The Riding School Connemara Pony

Elaine Heney

"Listening to the horse is the most important thing we can do"

Elaine Heney

First Edition Oct 2022 | Published by Grey Pony Films

www.greyponyfilms.com

Table of contents

About Elaine Heney

Elaine Heney is an Irish horsewoman, film producer at Grey Pony Films, #1 best-selling author, and director of the award-winning 'Listening to the Horse™' documentary. She has helped over 120,000+ horse owners in 113 countries to create great relationships with their horses. Elaine's mission is to make the world a better place for the horse. She lives in Ireland with her horses Ozzie & Matilda. Find all Elaine's books at www.writtenbyelaine.com

Online horse training courses

Discover our series of world-renowned online groundwork, riding, training programs and apps. Visit Grey Pony Films & learn more: www.greyponyfilms.com

Chapter 1

Ciara knotted her fingers into the little bay pony's black mane and buried her head into the soft coat of her neck, the tears spilling down her cheeks uncontrollably. She stifled a sob, trying desperately not to be heard by any of the other riders outside in the yard. The little pony snuggled into her, almost pulling her closer.

"I don't want to go Misty," she said in a whisper, not daring to speak any louder. She knew if she did she'd cry loud enough for the whole riding school to hear and she didn't want that. Someone would come to see if she was ok and this was private. She swallowed back her tears, trying to gulp in enough air that she didn't sob.

How could this be happening? How could it be real? Ciara's world hadn't been perfect, but it had been good and it had been hers and now it seemed like it had been smashed into a million pieces. Slowly she untangled her fingers from the mare's mane. This was it. The last ride at Fairbanks Riding School. The last ride on Misty. A fresh wave of tears rolled down Ciara's cheeks.

"Why do we have to move?" she managed to say through gritted teeth. "I want to stay here, with you." The little mare looked at her with knowing, dark brown eyes. It made Ciara's heart break even more.

Ciara's thoughts turned back to the looming moving day that was rapidly approaching. It didn't seem like five minutes ago that she had found out her life was being changed without her having any say in the matter.

Dad had come home looking so excited and happy. She remembered seeing him open the front door and step into the living room with a huge grin on his face. He'd run over and picked up Mum twirling her around and Ciara had been happy, she'd assumed something really good was happening. She rested her head on Misty's neck as she remembered the rest of that evening.

Mum and Dad had started talking. Ciara couldn't hear what they said, Dad was whispering, but from her vantage point on the stairs, she could see them in the little kitchen. Mum didn't look as happy as Dad was, her smile had faded and she'd put the salad bowl she'd been carrying down on the black marble counter shaking her head. Dad had taken her hands in his and started explaining something, but she still didn't look convinced.

That's when she'd started to worry. She'd slipped back upstairs into the little bedroom she shared with her younger sister and sat down on the white wooden framed bed wondering what was going on. Maddy was playing with her stuffed animals on the floor, making them tea, she'd looked up and frowned at Ciara.

"What's wrong?" she'd asked.

"I don't know," Ciara had replied. She remembered looking around the candy pink walls thinking how much she disliked the colour of them. It had been Maddy's choice really, but she'd agreed to make her sister happy. Now that they were leaving though, now that the room wouldn't be theirs, the walls seemed perfect and she'd miss them.

It had been an hour later when Mum and Dad called them all downstairs to tell them what was going on. They had sat down around the little light wooden dining table Mum had somehow managed to squeeze between the living room and the tiny kitchen. Her brother, Branden, had been unimpressed at being summoned downstairs. He kept repeating he was missing band practise and asking if Mum and Dad forgot that they had their first gig in a few weeks. Mum had glanced over at Dad then. She looked worried and Ciara didn't know why.

"Dad has some news," Mum had said slowly.

"What?" Branden had asked, sceptically.

"I've been offered a promotion," Dad said.

Branden had beamed. "That's great, does that mean we're going to rent a bigger place? Could we get somewhere with a garage or something, somewhere the band can practise? Oh, man, if we have a yard can I put a hoop up?"

"It's a little more complicated, Branden," Mum had said solemnly.

"Why?" Ciara had asked.

"Well," Dad said. "I'd need to be in the US for a year."

There was a murmur from around the table as everyone objected. Branden had started talking about the band, Maddy about her friends and school, but Ciara had just sat there thinking one thing. She was going to have to leave Misty.

"Wait, wait," Branden held up his hands. "Hold up, you said *you,* had to be in the States. What about us? What about Mum?"

"We're not sure yet," Mum said.

"We need to talk about it," Dad added. "Together. It would be a mistake to turn the promotion down. It's the best shot I have at a better job and a huge pay rise. After a year I'd be able to work back in the UK and I'd be on triple what I am now. We could buy a house, not just rent."

Ciara had always liked the idea of them living somewhere permanent.

They had rented three houses so far that she could remember, all in the same city. Now though the idea made her feel a little sick. The best thing in her life was riding horses. Going every weekend to the little school just outside of town. Fairbanks was small and only had a few ponies, but it was friendly and welcoming, it felt like a home away from home to Ciara. Her best friend Olivia even went there too.

"You could all come with me," Dad was saying.

Mum was shaking her head a little. "Mitch, we talked about this. You're going to be moving around over there for a year overseeing different areas of the company. We'd either have to move every few months or you'd be gone most of the time. I'm not sure I can parent alone, tackle new schools, a new country... and the book, I'm never going to finish my writing." She bit her lip.

"Why don't we just stay here and Dad go?" Maddy asked. "He can come home on weekends?"

Dad had smiled at her. "Sorry kiddo, bit too far just to fly back on weekends."

"And we can't afford the rent on this place and one for Dad," Mum had added. "It's too expensive in the city."

"Won't the company cover it?" Branden asked.

Dad shook his head. "No, I asked. They'll pay relocation, but not rent."

"When?" Branden huffed.

"A month or two. I'm waiting to hear back from the big boss. Look, I know the timing isn't good," Dad said. "But this is an amazing opportunity."

"For who Dad," Branden had said, pushing his chair away from the table. "I gotta go, I have practise."

He'd stomped away towards the door not looking back even after Dad called to him. Ciara had winced as the front door slammed shut. Mum had stood up and walked a couple of paces into the kitchen. She lent on the countertop and bit her lip, she looked over at Dad.

"There's only one way," she said with a shrug. "If we do this, there's only one way. We'll go stay with Dad."

Everyone looked over at her, a little surprised. Ciara had only seen Grandad Pat a few times. He lived like a hermit on a farm somewhere further north along the coast. Ciara had been there once when she was young, but Dad wasn't a country person and they didn't visit often. Grandad Pat was the opposite; he hated the city and wouldn't leave the animals for more than a day, so mostly the only contact there had been through cards and small gifts at Christmas time and on birthdays. Maddy had once asked why they didn't video chat and Mum had said Grandad Pat didn't have a phone or a computer to do it on, though Ciara wasn't sure she believed it. Everyone had a phone, right?

"Your Dad's?" Dad repeated.

Mum smiled. "It's perfect. Dad could do with the help around the farm. The kids would have lots of space, I can write and Dad will be there to help out if the children need anything. Plus, he's rattling around in that house all alone, and think about it Mitch, he's the only grandparent they have and they never see him."

Dad was nodding his head. "Ok, ok, call Pat, see if he's ok with it."

And just like that, it had been settled. No more consultation with them. Mum and Dad didn't even wait until Branden got home before calling Grandad. It had been sorted.

Ciara and Maddy had gone upstairs when Mum picked up the phone, walking up the beige carpet, their hands trailing on the smooth white bannister. Ciara had felt totally numb.

Once in their bedroom, she'd sat down on her bed and stared around at her things feeling lost. She'd picked up her stuffed toy dog that still sat on her bed, even though at twelve she felt a little too old to sleep with it at times. She'd hugged it to her as she looked past the picture of her and Misty on the bedside table to the rosettes, she had won at the little gymkhana the riding school had held the summer before.

Maddy had picked up her favourite rabbit toy from the tea party set up and sat down on her own bed on the opposite side of the room. Ciara had looked up when she'd heard a sniffle. Maddy had been crying but trying not to. Ciara knew exactly how she felt, maybe for different reasons, but the heartache was the same. She slipped off the bed and crossed the room wrapping one arm around her little sister.

"We still have a couple of months," Ciara said, trying to sound reassuring. "At least we get to stay until the start of the six weeks holidays."

Maddy had only cried harder. She'd curled into a little ball around Belinda Bunny and Ciara had found herself curling up around Maddy, lying together trying to understand what had just happened to their lives. Dad was going to be gone for a year. They were going to move somewhere new and probably in with a Grandad none of them had spent much time with, but worse than all of that she was going to have to stop going to Fairbanks and riding Misty.

Ciara brought herself back to reality. What had been months off at that moment with Maddy was here now. This was the last week of term. Next Saturday, instead of coming to Fairbanks and mounting Misty for an hour's lesson with Mrs. Barron, she'd be in the car heading away from the little bay pony.

She swallowed hard looking at Misty standing in her little stable, munching hay from the familiar red net. Ciara wasn't sure what it was about Misty that made her so special, but she was sure there would never be another pony in her life that made her feel quite the same. Most riding schools made the kids learning at them ride an array of horses to learn how different horses feel, move and react. The same was true at Fairbanks, but almost every lesson Ciara had taken there since she had first sat on Misty had been on the little bay Connemara. The first moment she had sat on her, they just fit, like two jigsaw puzzle pieces. Ciara knew it and so did Mrs. Barron. Sure, on occasion she rode another of the ponies and it was always fun to ride, but it was never the same. Something just felt off when she wasn't partnered with Misty and now that wouldn't happen anymore.

"Ciara?" Mrs. Barron said from outside the stable. Ciara looked up and realised the teacher wasn't looking in the stable. She had lent her back against the door and was looking out over the yard, giving her some privacy. "Your Mum's here sweetheart."

"Thanks," Ciara managed to say.

"You know, you can come to visit any time you like," Mrs. Barron said and Ciara thought for a second as her voice wavered. "I know it's hard sweetie, I've had to move on from horses too. It isn't easy, but I promise Misty will be well looked after and I know Olivia will keep you up to date on her."

Mrs. Barron pushed herself up off the wall of the stable. "I'll leave you alone for a minute." She started to move and then stopped glancing just a little over her shoulder. "Don't let this stop you riding though ok sweetie? You're too nice with the horses, too good to stop."

She smiled slightly and walked away leaving Ciara alone again with Misty. Ciara wrapped her arms around the pony's neck and held them there for a second hoping time would suddenly stop and she'd never have to let go. Eventually though, with a deep breath, she unwrapped her arms, kissed Misty's cheek, and slowly walked to the stable door.

As she slid the bolt open and slipped out into the yard, she looked back at Misty and felt her heartache. It took everything she had to close the door and push the bolt back into place.

"Bye Misty," she said, fighting back tears. "I'll miss you so much."

Ciara's tears threatened to spill again and she felt her lips quiver, blinking hard and sniffing. She spun around and dashed for the car park hoping no one would see her go. Mum's estate car was sat in the car park and Ciara forced herself to fight off her tears. She would cry at home in her room rather than in the car, for some reason she didn't want to, in front of Mum or Dad. Maybe it was because she blamed them for this, even though she knew they had their reasons for going ahead with the move, they were still the ones taking her away from Misty.

She pulled open the door and slid into the passenger seat not looking up. She grabbed the seat belt and fastened it trying not to sniffle even though her nose was running a little and felt tickly.

"Did you have a good lesson?" Mum asked, trying to sound cheerful.

"Sure," Ciara replied quietly.

"I know it's going to be hard," Mum said. "It'll be hard on all of us, but it'll be alright, you'll see."

Ciara wanted to yell and ask how it was going to be ok, but all she did was shrug. After all the tears, and the headache of that goodbye, she suddenly felt as though she could sleep for a thousand years. Mum reversed the car and pulled out of the car park. Ciara looked back out of the window just in time to see Misty's head pop out over the door, trailing hay over it as she went. Please, Ciara thought, please don't be the last time I ever see you. Mum turned out onto the road and suddenly Misty was gone out of sight, replaced by houses as Mum drove away back towards home. No, not home anymore, in six days somewhere else would become home, or at least would become the place they lived.

Chapter 2

Ciara pulled the white front door to their little house open, shoved her little black riding boots down by the coat rack, and ran for her bedroom as fast as she could, her tears already starting to spill. She heard Mum come in and call her name, but she ignored her and ran into her room.

Maddy was out at her friend's playing, probably for the last time, Ciara realised fleetingly. The thought made her feel even more angry and upset than she had been a second ago. It wasn't just her that was having a 'last thing' that day, Maddy was too. She threw herself onto her bed face down, glad Maddy wasn't there to see her cry. Ciara always tried to not look too upset when her little sister was around. She almost felt like she couldn't be - like she had to be the strong one because she was older.

She turned a little and caught sight of the picture of Misty on the bedside table. Seeing her own smiling face and Misty all brushed and neat, rosettes pinned to her bridle, made Ciara's chest hurt. She scrunched her pillow up and sobbed into it.

There was a knock at the door and Ciara lifted her head just enough to say "Go away." She didn't want to see Mum, not right then. It was their fault she'd never see Misty again.

The door opened anyway and Ciara looked around ready to shout she wanted to be alone, but it wasn't Mum in the doorway. Branden stepped into her room and wandered over to the bed. Ciara sat up and shuffled back in her bed, pulling her knees up under her chin and wiping her eyes on the sleeve of her blue jumper as he sat down.

"You ok?" he asked, nudging her lower leg with his elbow.

Ciara went to say yes but shook her head instead. Branden opened one arm and waved her over to him. She scooted over the bed and sat next to him while he put his arm around her and pulled her into a hug. For a while they just sat there being miserable together, no one saying a thing.

"Branden," she said eventually.

"Yeah?"

"Dad's not going to change his mind is he?" she said, realising she never thought it was going to happen, not really. She'd been imagining something would happen to stop the move, that Dad would turn around and say he was kidding, or that the promotion had been cancelled.

"No, sorry, I don't think that's going to happen," he said.

She leaned her head on his shoulder for another few minutes. He squeezed her shoulder and stood up. "I guess we should pack."

Ciara looked around her room feeling overwhelmed by everything. "I don't know where to start."

Branden nodded his head. "I'll get you some boxes."

He paused at the door and looked over at her. "I want to say it'll be ok."

Ciara swallowed. "I know," she replied. "I wanted to say the same thing to Maddy, but I couldn't."

He smiled at her and nodded. "I'll grab the boxes."

He'd only been gone a few minutes when Ciara heard the front door shut and the sound of running feet on the stairs. The door to the room flew open and Maddy ran in crying, throwing herself on her own bed, just like Ciara had done. Ciara picked up Belinda Bunny from the floor where she had fallen and passed it to Maddy. Maddy grabbed the rabbit and stuffed it under her arm without even lifting her head from the pillow.

Ciara thought about trying to comfort her as Branden had, but she knew Maddy needed a few minutes alone first. She rubbed Maddy's back a little before heading towards the door to get the boxes from Branden.

She made it to the top of the stairs before she heard Branden talking to Dad. Her brother sounded more than a little angry. Ciara crept to the top of the staircase and peered down.

"Branden, we've talked about this, this is the best thing for our family," Dad was saying. Ciara pressed herself against the white railings so she could see Dad standing in the living room, his hands on his hips. Branden stood opposite him, he ran his hands through his short dark hair.

"Really? Best for the family Dad, or best for you?" he said. "You don't get it, do you? You think everyone can just up and go! You want to know what this move means to our family? Huh? It means Ciara is upstairs sobbing because she'll never see that pony, Misty again." Ciara pulled back from the railing, she never knew Branden had known about Misty, let alone her name. He had come to the little gymkhana, but he hadn't stayed too long. It surprised her.

"And Maddy, Maddy had nightmares all week," Branden went on, pointing upstairs to make his point clearer. That was true, Maddy had crept into Ciara's bed all week, but she hadn't realised anyone else in the house had.

"Branden…" Dad started, but Branden cut him off.

"And me, well, I don't have band practise anymore, because I'm not in the band. You can't have a gig without a guitarist, can you!"

"Branden…" Dad tried again.

"Save it," Branden said, picking up his basketball from the back of the couch. "I'll be back for tea Mum," he said as he walked towards the door tossing the ball.

As the door closed behind her brother, Ciara watched as her Mum stepped into the living room. Dad looked really sad.

"Mitch," Mum shook her head. "We have to tell him."

"No," Dad replied. "The kids don't need to know."

"Look, I know you think this is protecting them Mitch, but it's not. We need to tell them, at least Branden, he's old enough," Mum said.

"Laura," Dad said, sitting down on the grey armchair in the corner of the room.

"Mitch there's nothing wrong with being honest with them," Mum said crouching down beside the chair. "If they know this is the only way."

"What, tell them it's promotion or nothing, that the company restructures would mean my job doesn't exist? Laura, you know how worried we were before they offered me that chance. This is a gift for us."

"I know," Mum said. "That's my point," she smiled. "They don't see it that way because they don't know the full story. We should tell them."

Dad reached out and pulled Mum into a hug. "I don't think it would change anything. It won't change what's happening and they might worry that my job is at risk still. It's better this way," Dad said.

Ciara pulled back from the stairs and sat on the landing, her mind racing. Was it true? Did Dad not have a choice? The idea bounced around her head. Either way, they would probably have had to move, or even if they hadn't, chances are they wouldn't have been able to afford to let her keep riding for a while. She wondered if she should tell Maddy and Branden what she had overheard. She thought about it for a second and then shook her head. It wasn't her secret to tell.

"I'm going to run these boxes up to the girls," Ciara heard Mum say. She scrabbled over the floor back to her room, not wanting Mum to know she'd been listening in.

Maddy looked up at her with red-rimmed eyes. Ciara smiled at her and sat down on the end of the bed.

"Last time playing with Marie?" Ciara asked.

Maddy nodded. Marie and Maddy had been best friends for as long as Ciara could remember, she'd been the one to give them the nickname the M&M's.

"She's going on holiday tomorrow." Maddy sniffed. "She'll not be at school for my last week."

"She can come and visit," Ciara said, trying to smile. "No way the M&M's aren't going to be together again."

Mum opened the door with an armful of boxes. Seeing both girls sat together, she put the boxes down on Ciara's bed and sat with them, pulling both into a hug.

"It's going to be ok girls, it is, I promise," Mum said.

Ciara wanted to ask how, but stopped herself, remembering what Dad and Mum had been talking about a few minutes before. Somehow hearing their conversation had stolen Ciara's anger, if not her sorrow.

"Mum," Maddy asked in a small voice. "Marie can come to visit right?"

"Of course, she can," Mum said, squeezing Maddy's shoulder.

"And Ciara can still ride?" Maddy asked, making Ciara smile.

"I hope so," Mum said. "We'll have to find out if there's a riding school close by," she smirked. "Heck, Grandad might even have horses again when we get there."

Ciara looked confused. It was the first time Mum had mentioned horses at the farm. Grandad always talked about things like chickens and a few sheep, but not horses. "Grandad had horses?"

"Yes," Mum said, smiling and frowning at Ciara. "You don't remember?" Ciara shook her head. "Well, you know that picture of you sat on the big grey horse?"

Ciara nodded, she knew the picture well. It was sat in a frame on the small sideboard. It showed her sitting on a huge grey horse, held in place by a smiling Grandad. Branden was sitting behind her, his arms around her waist, while Mum stood beside them holding a baby Maddy. She'd always thought it was at a fair or something.

"That's Grandad's old horse. Max they called him, erm, Maximums II. Gosh, he loved that horse," Mum smiled. "That was probably the last time we were at the farm. I think Max passed away about a year later, he was old though," Mum added.

"And now he has another horse?" Ciara asked curiously.

Mum took a deep breath. "I don't know. He said he wasn't getting another horse after Max, he was adamant for years, but lately, I don't know, I think he misses having horses around the farm. He keeps saying he's looking."

Ciara glanced over at the picture of Misty on the nightstand. She could imagine how Grandad had felt losing Max. She swallowed hard.

"Anyway," Mum said with a smile. "I brought some boxes up and some bubble wrap. Pack up anything non-essential ok? You can keep Belinda Bunny and Ruff out though, things like that," Mum said, glancing from the rabbit to Ciara's floppy-looking dog. Mum giggled. "Ruff is looking a bit rough."

Ciara scowled at her and snatched the dog up from her bed in a hug. "That's mean," she said but smiled, just a little at Mum.

"It's going to be ok girls, really, it will be," she said. "I know it doesn't feel like it, but we'll make this work."

Mum stepped out of the room. Ciara glanced at Maddy and then followed her out onto the landing.

"Mum?" Ciara said.

Mum turned around with a smile. "Yes, sweetie?"

Ciara walked over and hugged Mum around the waist. "I heard what Dad said," she admitted.

"Oh, sweetheart," Mum said, hugging her back.

"I won't say anything," Ciara added. "But, I think you should tell Branden too." Mum nodded with a smile.

Ciara let go and walked back to her room. She picked up a box, the cardboard feeling thick and chunky in her fingers. Absently she packed up some of the things on her bedside table before turning to look at the rosettes stuck up on the wall. Carefully, gently, she pulled them off one by one, running the shiny bright ribbons through her fingers as she carefully placed them in the box. The last one she took down she turned over, reading the words she had written on the back, Misty, fancy dress, and the gymkhana date.

With a sigh, she put it in the box and looked at the last items on the table, a little lamp, and her photo with Misty.

Anything non-essential Mum had said. Ciara folded the lid on the box closed and put it down by the door next to the one Maddy had packed up. She turned around and looked at their almost bare bedroom and fought the urge to cry again. Maddy walked over to her, Belinda Bunny hanging by one ear, and took hold of her hand. Ciara looked down at her and smiled, squeezing her hand a little.

"Maybe Misty can visit too?" Maddy suggested. "I bet Grandad wouldn't mind her coming too."

The thought made Ciara smile, even though it wasn't likely to happen. "Maybe," Ciara replied.

Chapter 3

Ciara flopped down on the little green picnic bench that sat under the big oak tree outside of school. She hadn't felt very hungry at lunch and barely ate her sandwich. The other kids were playing in the yard, but all she could think about was that this was her last day. The last time she would see her school, the last day she'd have lunch in the cafeteria and in a few minutes, she'd have her last class with Miss Fields. Then it would be home for the last dinner they'd have as a family for a while and the last night in her room. She sighed sadly.

She felt tears fill her eyes and wiped them away not wanting anyone at school to see her upset. For a few moments she sat there wondering what it would be like just to stand up and walk away. Run from all the lasts, be free. In her daydream she saw herself walking out through the school gates and heading down the street back to her house. No one would be home; it would be easy to let herself in. Take the things out of her rucksack and replace it with some clothes and important things.

There was a bus stop just along the road. The number 26 went right into town and from there Ciara knew there was a bus that arrived, 20 minutes later, just outside of Fairbanks. Ciara imagined herself hopping on and then arriving at the riding school, stood outside the stables with the backpack on one shoulder. What would she do? She could of course slip inside, find Misty's tack and they could run away together. Just keep riding from place to place. The idea made Ciara smile, but she knew it was a silly thought, both she and Misty would need to eat, to rest, not to mention the fact that she would be stealing Misty. Maybe she could just hide at the school? Sleep in the barn, sure it would be cold at night in the winter, but she wouldn't have to leave Misty. Her thoughts made her smile sadly. She was doing it again, pretending it would be alright, that there was some way out of the mess, even though there wasn't. If she ran away to be with Misty she'd be leaving Mum, Dad, Branden and Maddy.

"Hey?" Olivia said, throwing her bag onto the table and sitting down on it, resting her boots on the bench next to Ciara.

Ciara looked up and tried to smile, but she knew Oliva would see straight through her. "This sucks." She huffed, pulling her hands into the sleeves of her jacket.

Olivia nodded, tucking her loose blonde hair behind her ears. "Well, yes, yes it does."

She climbed down off the table and sat next to Ciara putting her arm around her shoulder. "This is the last day I get my best friend in the same school."

Ciara shook her head. "Sorry, I keep forgetting it sucks for you too."

"Have you come up with another wild plan to stop the move yet?" Olivia asked with a smile, it was like she could see into Ciara's head.

Ciara shook her head. "Maybe run away and live in the barn at Fairbanks?"

"Oooh," Olivia smiled. "I could bring you food once a week smuggled in my riding hat."

Ciara smiled and nudged her friend. "I don't want to go Liv."

"I know," Olivia said, tightening her hug. "But at least we can call each other, right? I mean your Grandad's place has a phone, yes?"

Ciara smiled. "Phone, yes, internet not so much."

"Really?" Olivia's mouth fell open.

"Really," Ciara replied.

"But you're getting the internet. I mean, you have to get the internet, it's like the law or something," Oliva stated. Ciara shrugged. "Oh, it's like you're moving to a mountain top or some remote island. Who doesn't have the internet?"

"Grandad apparently. Mum says he had horses though, when she was little," Ciara said.

"Really?" Olivia smiled. "And the farm's by the beach, right?"

Ciara nodded. She had to admit that the farm sounded nice, the idea of being surrounded by fields and sandy beaches, able to watch the waves. It would have sounded fantastic if she were visiting for a few weeks, it was the fact it wasn't just a visit, they were staying.

"Well, that's something. I'd love to live by the sea." She shook her blonde hair. "Swimming in the ocean in the summer, watching winter storms blow in," she sighed.

"You'll come and visit, right?" Ciara asked, her voice sounding smaller than she had intended.

Olivia nodded. "And I promise I'll make sure Misty is ok," she added.

"Thanks," Ciara said looking down at the picnic bench so she didn't cry again.

Olivia looked at her with a frown. "This isn't right, your last night. We should be doing something cool. Hit the cinema, binge on popcorn and ice cream."

Ciara tried to smile. "Dad's getting pizza. He wants us all to have a final family dinner together before his flight tomorrow and our drive up to the farm."

Olivia narrowed her eyes, a smile spreading over her face. "We could sneak out and meet up."

Ciara laughed knowing neither would do such a thing and Olivia smiled. Then her face lit up, the way it always did when she had an idea. "Give me Branden's phone number," she said suddenly pulling out a biro with no lid from her multicoloured woven backpack and rolling up her sleeve so Ciara could write on her arm. Olivia had a tendency to lose things and if it was important to her, she tended to make a note of it somewhere it couldn't be misplaced. It made Ciara chuckle.

"You want my brother's phone number?" she teased.

Olivia slapped her arm and Ciara faked an OW. "Ew, he's your brother, I mean he's cute and in a band, so maybe, but brother, no!" Olivia garbled.

"Oh, that's right, you like Will in class 5," Ciara said with a grin watching Olivia's face turn red.

"Yarg, no way," Olivia said, but hid her face a little behind the blond waves. "It was Nate."

Ciara shook her head and took the pen writing Branden's number on her arm. "Either way I don't get it," she said.

"When you're older you will." Olivia replied.

Ciara stifled a laugh. "You're only a few months older than me!" It was true, Olivia was the oldest in their class, while Ciara was the youngest, but there wasn't that much of an age gap between them. Olivia rolled her sleeve down over the number.

"Ok, make sure you're with Branden about 7.30 tonight, ok?" she said.

Ciara nodded, the fun of the last few minutes had almost made her forget what was happening, but when Olivia mentioned tonight, the memories came flooding back and Ciara's face fell. Their last lunch time was nearly over. Her last night was speeding towards her far too quickly. With a sigh Ciara took her school button off her blazer and looked at it. The little pin badge was an important part of their uniform. Everyone had to wear it on either their blue blazer or on their tie, if they chose to wear one. Most of the girls didn't, preferring just their plaid skirt, a shirt and the blazer. Oliva was terrible for forgetting her badge. Their head master had even thrown her in detention a couple of times for not having it on for a whole week straight.

Ciara turned the little pin over in her hands, looking at the golden coloured falcon surrounded by an enamelled blue circle with the school name printed around it. She smiled and flipped open the pin, fixing it on Olivia's bag. The blonde girl looked at her confused.

"Don't you want to keep it?" she asked. "Like a memento of this." She looked around her, holding up her hands.

"You can give me it back when we both graduate," Ciara said. "Until then it can keep you out of detention."

Olivia smiled. "Promise. When we graduate and we buy a farm together and have lots of horses, I will return your badge."

They sat huddled together on the picnic bench. At that moment their daydream of running a horse farm seemed very far away indeed.

*

"Ciara, Maddy, the pizza is here," Mum called upstairs.

Ciara glanced over at Maddy and sighed. They stood up together and headed quietly towards the door. In the doorway Ciara looked back at their room. It seemed bare without their books, Maddy's toys and her posters. The removal men would be there to collect the boxes first thing in the morning and Mum had insisted they have everything ready to go except for their pyjamas and bedding that night, though Belinda Bunny and Ruff were still unpacked. Ciara felt Maddy take hold of her hand. She looked down at her sister and tried to smile as they turned and trudged towards the stairs.

The smell of pizza usually made everyone happy, but not that night. Downstairs was as bare except for the sofa, TV and boxes. Ciara and Maddy padded into the kitchen to see Mum trying to be upbeat and failing. Ciara knew she was going to miss Dad and that he would miss them, but part of her couldn't feel sorry for them, as much as she knew Dad's reasons for moving them all, she still felt he was to blame for taking her away from Misty and Olivia. At least she could explain it to Olivia though, she could only hope Misty understood. Ciara realised one of the things that was bothering her most was the thought that Misty might not understand what had happened, that she would wonder where Ciara had gone. That the pony would miss her and think she had done something wrong to make Ciara go away. The thoughts made her heart ache anew.

"Here you go sweetie," Mum said, passing a little box to Maddy. "It's just cheese."

Maddy took the box without a smile, turned and wandered away into the living room silently. She sat down on the floor near Brandon, snuggling into his legs. Her brother glanced down at the little figure sat staring at the TV and glanced over at Mum. She swallowed hard. Maddy had been quiet around both Mum and Dad since the previous weekend, so quiet even Ciara was worried about her.

"Ciara," Mum said. "You wanted mushroom, right?"

Ciara nodded. "Thanks Mum," she said taking the box and heading into the living room to sit by Branden.

Dad jogged down the stairs with a smile that faded when he saw them sat silently together. "Come on troops," he tried. "Last night together for a bit, what should we do, play a game, watch a film?"

"You packed the games," Branden said flatly without looking up.

"And the films," Ciara added, but she at least tried to smile and look in his direction.

"Well, maybe there's something on TV?" he suggested picking up the remote.

Mum came in carrying her own pizza and sat in one of the two chairs while Dad flicked through the channels. Eventually he settled on an old film Ciara wasn't interested in, but she watched it anyway, picking at her pizza.

"What, is no one hungry?" Dad asked.

No one answered. Ciara wondered absently what time it was, the clock that usually hung on the wall had been packed away and she didn't have a watch. Just as she thought about asking Dad or Branden, a buzzing sound filled the room. Branden frowned.

"Turn it off Brand, it's family time," Dad said.

Branden pulled his phone out and stared at it. "I don't even know the number," he said.

"It's Olivia!" Ciara beamed, making a grab for the phone. Branden pulled it out of her reach and raised an eyebrow. "I'm sorry, I know I should have asked first, but..."

He smiled at her, unlocked it and passed her his phone. "It's ok. This time."

Ciara pressed the green button on the screen and Olivia's face flashed into view. "Hey, for a second there I thought you gave me a fake number or something," she giggled.

"Where are you?" Ciara asked, realising she was outside.

Olivia beamed. "I thought you might like to see someone." She turned her phone around and Ciara instantly knew where she was.

There were the little green painted stables with their slate-coloured roofs, the yard full of horses just finishing a lesson.

Olivia was walking now, heading across the yard to a stable Ciara knew well. A few steps away from the stall Misty's head popped out and Ciara felt her heart skip a beat.

"Misty," she said quietly.

The little bay mare whickered and Ciara was certain it was because she had said her name. Olivia turned so she was stood next to the stable and Ciara was able to see both her and Misty.

"It's your last night, it seemed like you should get a chance to say bye." Olivia said with a sad smile. Misty nudged her. "I have a carrot, hold on." Olivia said, making Ciara half laugh half cry.

"Thanks," she said, trying not to sob.

"We promise we will send pictures won't we," Olivia said as Misty nudged her again. "You can tell your brother to show you them, right Branden?" she shouted the last part.

Branden took his phone for a moment and looked at Olivia. Ciara could just imagine her smiling at him defiantly. "Do not clog my phone with horse pictures," he said.

"You can delete them as soon as Ciara has seen them or when she gets her own phone." Oliva's voice filtered through the speaker.

Branden rolled his eyes and handed Ciara back his phone, she saw him smile a little though as he did and knew any pictures Olivia sent she'd see.

"Ok, I have a lesson in five, so I'm sorry I have to cut this short."

"Thanks for doing it," Ciara said.

"No problem at all," Olivia said, her face suddenly grew serious. "I'm going to miss you."

"Me too," Ciara said. "Bye Misty." She waved and Oliva waved back before the phone went black. Ciara handed the phone back to Branden and looked at her pizza, she wasn't sure she could eat another bite that night.

Chapter 4

Ciara stared out of the window as the green field sped by. They had dropped Dad off at the airport early that morning, Mum had tried not to look upset, but they all knew she was. Even Branden had looked a little misty-eyed as Dad headed through the security gates. They had hung around for a while until his plane had taken off and then headed to the car and set off themselves for Grandad's.

The drive had been a quiet one, no one felt like chatting or even listening to music, though Branden had put some on. Mum had said they'd be at the farm for tea time but stopped at a little café with a play park next to it for lunch. Usually, that would have made Maddy very happy, but she didn't even ask to go in and try the swings. Worse, when they had sat down at a little booth to order, Ciara had spotted a girl around her age riding a bay pony in the field across the road. Cantering in circles and popping over little cross poles. It made Ciara think of Misty and for a second she imagined that was them jumping.

Mum had said it was only another couple of hours' drive to Grandad's and from then on things would be a little more rural. If anything, though, Ciara thought, that was an understatement. They passed through the occasional small village, but there were mostly just fields and trees.

"Look, there's the sea," Mum said, trying to sound excited.

Ciara looked absently out of the window on Maddy's side of the car. Sure, enough there was a stretch of sea just beyond some scrubby-looking grass and deep red-brown cliffs, the dark waves topped with white foam.

"It's nicer near Grandads," Mum said when no one commented. "You could go swimming maybe, as long as me or Branden are there, ey Brand."

"Whatever," Branden replied, putting his headphones in and flicking something up on his phone.

They drove on, hugging the coastline, and gradually the sharp cliffs gave way to dunes of green and yellow grasses, with glimpses of soft golden sands. Ciara caught sight of someone on a chestnut pony cantering along the sands and watched them for a while. She couldn't make out much about the rider, but the pony's coat shone brightly in the sun, their head held high, tail held up and streaming out behind them. From the high tail and the dished face, Ciara assumed it was an Arab, it was certainly going at some speed across the damp, wave-washed shore. It both made Ciara smile and feel sad.

A few minutes later Mum slowed down and Ciara realised they had arrived. Mum drove through an old white gate that had rusted in parts and didn't look like it had been closed in years. On it was hung a white sign with black letters that read Rook Cove Farm. The driveway they pulled onto was little more than a stone track, and the car bumbled along it slowly towards a large, grey stone house with a green front door. It looked a little dull, perhaps, Ciara thought, even spooky. Maddy reached her hand out and took Ciara's and Ciara squeezed it reassuringly.

To one side of the house was another stone building which she realised was a barn and two stables. To Ciara's surprise, as they drew closer, a grey horse's head popped out of the furthest stable, shortly followed by a second one from the stable next door. The first horse let out a little shout and, a moment later, Grandad appeared around the side of the building with a blue wheelbarrow full of hay. He put the barrow down and waved as Mum pulled past him and parked up outside the house. Grandad dusted his hands off and walked towards the car as they began to clamber out. Mum went to hug him with a smile.

"Hi Dad," she said with a smile.

"Got here ok then," he smiled. "Stuff got here earlier, I put the boxes in the right rooms."

"Thanks, Dad," Mum said. "And thanks for having us."

Grandad waved her thanks away and shook Branden's hand. "Branden, look at you, might need a haircut there," he smiled looking at Branden's shaggy hair, Branden rolled his eyes but smiled when he saw Grandad smirking.

"Now, hang on," Grandad said, looking around. "Aren't we missing one? I see Branden and Ciara, but where's Maddy?" he pretended to look in the car and, on the roof, while Maddy hid behind Ciara giggling a little. Finally, he dived around the side of Ciara and caught her up in a hug. She squealed and laughed; all traces of nerves gone. Grandad spun her around before putting her down and looking at Ciara.

"Oh, now then, that can't be Ciara?" Grandad said, squinting at her. "Not this young lady?"

Ciara smiled. She hadn't expected Grandad to be so jolly, it seemed surprising considering he lived alone. One of the horses started to kick the door and Ciara looked over at it tossing its head up and down. Now she was outside the car Ciara realised it was a big horse, much larger than the ones she had met at Fairbanks. Grandad saw her looking and smiled.

"That's Louie and Aramis," Grandad said. "You want to meet them, I could do with a hand giving them some hay." He raised his voice a little. "Isn't that right Louie, stop banging the door." Ciara smiled.

"You go on in Laura, I'll be there in a second, just borrowing this one," he said smiling as he put a hand on Ciara's shoulder.

"Alright," Mum said with a smile. "Branden, grab some bags sweetie."

As Branden began to help Mum unload the boot of the car. Ciara followed Grandad across the cobbled yard towards the stables. The stonework was patched and the green doors a little flakey, but the building looked much more solid than the timber stables at Fairbanks. Louie watched them come over eagerly, his ears flicking back and forth.

"He's the young one," Grandad said. "Only four aren't you?" Grandad rubbed Louie's nose and then grabbed some hay from the barrow. "Open the door will you?"

Ciara unlatched the door and Louie gave it a gentle nudge but didn't try to come out. He was massive compared to Ciara but was so sweet and young, that he almost seemed smaller. He stuffed his nose in the general area of Ciara's pockets and snuffled around with his pink nose.

"Give over," Grandad said, pushing in with an armful of hay. "She hasn't got anything for you."

Louie flicked his ears at Ciara again hopefully and then, when no carrots appeared, followed Grandad over to the metal hay rack he had filled and started munching.

"He's so big," Ciara said.

"He's not done growing yet either," Grandad smiled. "He's an Irish draught, same as Aramis. Come on, I'll introduce you."

Grandad bolted Louie back in and they stepped to the stable next door. Aramis's head appeared over the door and he regarded Ciara carefully. He seemed much more relaxed than Louie and maybe a little less eager. Grandad patted his neck.

"Aramis is five, he's a little older than Louie and much more aware of where his feet go, isn't that right?"

Aramis snorted a little and very gently nudged Grandad, before bending down to snuffle at Ciara who had stretched out her hand towards his soft grey muzzle. Ciara smiled.

"Much more of a gent," Grandad said. "You open the door and ask him to step back." Ciara looked at him confused. "Just say back."

Ciara unlatched the door while Grandad grabbed the hay. Stepping into the doorway Ciara looked up at Aramis. "Back," she said, her voice coming out a little smaller than she had hoped, but, to her surprise, Aramis lowered his head a little and took a step backward. Ciara smiled as did Grandad as he bustled in with his armful of hay.

"That's the way," Grandad smiled.

"Do you ride them?" Ciara asked, stepping up and patting Aramis's shoulder.

"Not yet," Grandad smiled. "You know a horse isn't physically mature until they're at least 5 and a half years of age at the earliest, and quite often they are even 6 or 7 years of age before they are fully grown. I suppose Louie could be backed now, but he wouldn't be ready to ride for a while. Aramis here, he's about ready to start I'd say. Maybe you could help." Grandad smiled.

Ciara beamed. "I'd like that," she said.

"Your Mum said you rode, there's school not too far away. Maybe once you're settled you could go down, take a look."

Ciara forced a smile even though the thought of riding only made her miss Misty. She focused on Aramis, stroking his soft grey coat. "Maybe," she said. Grandad seemed to sense something was bothering her, but she didn't want to talk about it.

Her mind thought back to the chestnut Arab she'd seen cantering on the beach. She wondered if it lived close by.

"Will you back Louie then, or just leave him until he's older?" Ciara asked.

"I'll see how he gets on. I suspect he'll be like Aramis, but each horse is different."

"What did you do with Aramis?" Ciara asked, still petting the horse.

"Well, I didn't back Aramis. He and Louie have only been here about six months, but I know the lady that bred them and she starts her horses the way I would. Aramis has had a bridle and saddle on and done work on the long lines but that's about all. Soon enough it'll be time to sit on and walk around a little. It's important to get them out a bit too, to see different things. I've had them both down the beach already, let them feel the sand and waves."

"Do you show them other things too?" Ciara asked. "I saw a video once with a lady holding an umbrella and walking her horse."

Grandad laughed a little. "Never thought of that, but yes, I'll show them tarps and such like. Time was I would take them up to the big local show, but that stopped a long while back."

Grandad patted Aramis's shoulder and Ciara smiled, as she made her way back to the stable door.

"Well, that'll be them alright for a bit. Let's go get you settled in." Grandad's face fell a little as he pushed the kick bolt on. "I'm afraid your room might not be to your taste, but I reckon we could paint it a bit, or put up some pictures so it feels more like home."

Ciara smiled and followed him across the stony yard towards the house, where Mum was still dropping off bags. She stepped through the green door into a rather dull-looking hallway. Ahead of her and just to one side was a stairway with an old-looking brown carpet and dusky pinkish walls. There were doors on either side of the stairway, both open.

"That's the living room," Grandad said pointing to the door on his left. Ciara poked her head into the room. It was large and warm looking, with a little TV and a huge fireplace with a wood burner in it. There was a green velvet-like sofa and chairs that looked as old as the house, but they were clean and comfortable looking. Behind them was a unit dominating the wall covered in glass things, pictures, and what looked to Ciara like rosettes.

"Dining room, don't go in there much," Grandad said pointing to the other door which was closed. "Kitchen's down there," Grandad said pointing down the hall.

Mum struggled past them with a bag of groceries and headed down the hallway. "We've put the kettle on." She called back over her shoulder and Ciara followed her towards the kitchen door while Grandad closed the front door.

The kitchen was big and dark, like everywhere else. The walls had been painted a creamy colour, but the place was dominated by a black range cooker and a wooden table covered with a brown tablecloth. The curtains were brown and cream and covered more of the window than they probably should have. Ciara glanced at Mum who shook her head a little.

"I know," Grandad said. "It could do with a coat of paint, but, well, that was Grandma's job."

Ciara could barely remember Granny, she wasn't sure Maddy had ever met her. The thought of the house being the same for so long made Ciara feel a little sad.

"So, where are we staying?" Branden asked, cutting through the uncomfortable silence that had fallen.

"Right, yes," Grandad said, clearing his throat. "You make a brew Laura, I'll show the young'uns around. Now, through that door," Grandad pointed to a dark wooden door next to the range. "That's the utility, boot room, whatever they call it these days, and the downstairs loo."

He headed out back into the hallway waving for them to follow. They trooped upstairs onto a small landing with six doors off it. Grandad stood in the middle. "That first door, that's my bedroom. Your Mum will have her old room, that's the one at the back. Middle door there, that's the bathroom. Branden, you're in that room." He pointed to a door opposite Mum's. "Sorry, it's not so big,"

Branden opened the door and Ciara strained to look inside. The room had been painted blue with a creamy carpet, a large dark wooden bed sat against the wall and a small wooden desk had been put under the window. It didn't look too much different from the size of the room Branden had before, if anything, Ciara thought it looked bigger.

"This is you, girls," Grandad said, pushing open a door.

The room beyond was pretty light. The walls were covered in cream wallpaper and light pink curtains were hung at the window and their beds from the old house had been set up already on either side of the room.

"The curtains were your Mum's. I thought it made the room a little more, well, nicer," he said with a smile.

Ciara and Maddy walked into the room. Ciara went over to the window and looked out, she could see the stables, the fields, and beyond that the sea. It was a lovely view.

"Can I have this one?" Maddy asked, sitting on one of the beds and bouncing on her bum a little. Ciara nodded and smiled.

"Well, I'll let you settle in. Dinner is at six," Grandad said. "Nothing too fancy I'm afraid, just some packet fish and chips and a few peas from the garden. Oh, hey, you haven't seen that yet. It's an old walled one at the side of the house, it's a bit overgrown down the back, but the veg patch is great. Your Mum's old playhouse is still down there, maybe we could tidy it up for you eh?"

Maddy smiled broadly. She'd always wanted a garden to plant flowers in ever since Dad had bought her a little fairy planter for their bedroom as a birthday present.

"Can we plant flowers?" she asked.

"Course you can," Grandad smiled. "Just not in my veg patch." She smiled at Ciara and for a second everything seemed alright.

Chapter 5

Sunshine gently filtered around the curtains making Ciara blink her eyes open. For a second she struggled to remember where she was. Slowly she sat up looking around the room. She and Maddy had unpacked a few things the night before, a couple of toys, and a few things that usually went on their nightstands. Ciara glanced over at the picture of her and Misty with a sigh, her eyes fell on her little bedside clock and she realised it was still early. Maddy turned over, snuggling back down under her duvet and Ciara wondered if she should do the same.

Usually, she had a lesson early on a Saturday morning and she needed to get up, but today there wasn't a reason to. She tried laying back down but found she couldn't sleep. She sat up again wondering if she should get a book, or maybe start unpacking her clothes into the huge dark wooden wardrobe that sat at the foot of her bed. That could wake Maddy up though and that didn't seem fair.

There was a creak from the landing, the sound of someone carefully closing a door. Ciara doubted it was Branden, he'd sleep until noon if given the chance. It had to be Mum or Grandad. Ciara slipped out of bed and grabbed the clothes she had left out the night before from on top of her suitcase and pulled them on as quietly as she could.

Maddy stirred a little and looked over at her with a yawn. "Ciara? What's going on?" she asked.

"Nothing, I just can't sleep. It's early though," Ciara smiled.

Maddy pulled her blankets up under her chin and yawned again as Ciara slipped out of the room into the hallway. She padded downstairs in her socks wondering where she had packed her novelty horse slippers Mum and Dad had given her for her birthday. The door to the dining room was closed, but the ones to the living room and kitchen were open.

Ciara hadn't been in the living room yet. The evening before they had sat in the kitchen for ages together, chatting to Grandad and hearing stories about Mum when she was little. Absently, Ciara pushed the living room door open wide and stepped inside. The little bit she had seen of it the day before had shown her it was very old-fashioned looking but comfortable and when she tested the couch, she found it was the softest she'd ever sat on. Ciara looked around herself a little more. There was a clock on the wall, with wooden triangles all around the golden-coloured face, like a strange-looking sun. Above the fire was a wooden sleeper on which sat several pictures, one of Grandad and Grandma, one of Mum, and one of Grandad with a big grey horse she recognised as Max.

Slowly she stood up and headed over to the dark wooden sideboard at the back of the room. There was a collection of glass paperweights on some of the shelves, each with different colours and bubbles in them. There were photographs here too, some of her, Branden and Maddy, even one of Mum and Dad when they got married, as well as several pictures of horses. A lot of them showed Grandad stood with them, rosettes pinned to their bridles, just like the picture of Misty. Ciara noticed a small trophy and some rosettes mounted on the frames too. She reached out and brushed her finger over the trophy.

"Ciara?" Ciara spun around to see Maddy standing in the doorway, her hair a tangled mess of curls.

"You scared me," Ciara smiled, stepping away from the cabinet. "How come you're up."

"I couldn't sleep either," she said, rubbing her eyes. "Where's Grandad?"

"In the kitchen," Grandad's voice wafted along the hallway. "If you're up you might as well have some breakfast and make yourselves useful."

Maddy smiled and ran off down the hallway, and with a look back at the trophy, Ciara followed. Grandad was making scrambled eggs on the range as they walked in, Grandad waved them towards chairs and they sat down together. The toast popped loudly from the toaster making Ciara jump and Maddy giggle. Grandad put plates down in front of them and passed over some butter and a knife to Ciara with a smile.

"Thanks," Ciara said, picking up some of the toast and buttering it for herself and Maddy.

"Eggs won't be long. There's juice in the fridge if you like," he added.

"I'll get it," Maddy said, jumping up.

Several minutes later Ciara found herself happily munching on the toast and eggs. Maddy was having seconds.

"These are the best," Maddy said around a mouth full of toast.

"Well, they're fresh that's why. When we've done, I'll take you out to the garden, and introduce you to the girls," Grandad said with a wink.

"Girls?" Ciara asked.

Grandad smiled. "Henrietta, Egglantine, Clucky, Birdie, and, well Chuck, he's an honorary girl." Grandad laughed, and Maddy looked confused. "Chickens."

Maddy's face brightened. "You have chickens."

"Sure do, and a couple of goats, Nanny, and Jilly. Oh, and there's Winston, Hattie, and Peach, they're the sheep," Grandad said.

"There are sheep!" Maddy said tugging on Ciara's arm.

Grandad laughed. "Oh, there used to be a lot more, had a whole flock, for their fleece, not for eating, ah, but they aren't what you call economical nowadays. Plus, the sheep were really Grans, the three left are the last ones she had."

"Can we feed them?" Maddy asked.

"That you can," Grandad said. "Be nice to have help around the place. Maybe you could be the head chicken feeder!"

"Yey!" Maddy said. "When can I start?"

"As soon as you get your coat and shoes." Grandad smiled. Maddy almost launched herself off her chair and rushed to the door. "Hold up kid!" Grandad called. "Boots and coats are in the boot room." He pointed a thumb at the door at the back of the kitchen.

Maddy spun on her heels and raced to the door, grabbing at Ciara as she went. "Come on, come on!"

Ciara smiled and stood up, following her sister to the door. The wood-panelled walls of the boot room were painted yellow, with hooks dotted along them, under which was a little bench with cubby holes for shoes or boots. Ciara spotted her coat and pulled it down, grabbing her black riding boots and pulling them on.

"Are we ready?" Grandad asked.

"Yes!" the girls chorused.

"Off we go then." He pushed open the back door and they stepped out into the sunshine. It had been a little late to properly explore the farm the night before and Ciara was excited to see what it looked like. Grandad led the way along a solid-looking wall to a little green door.

"This is the garden," he said. He turned the round metal knob slowly and swung open the door with a flourish.

Ciara and Maddy stepped inside and looked around. One end of the walled garden was divided up into neat, raised beds full of growing vegetables, behind which sat a large greenhouse. The other end though was a mess of what had once been flower beds and little pathways. At the very back was a gnarled old tree and a wooden summerhouse in desperate need of painting. Maddy's face faltered a little.

"I think you might need some help to sort the mess before you can plant anything," Grandad said looking at her face.

Ciara smiled. "I'll help."

"Thanks," Maddy smiled.

"Chickens," Grandad said.

He stepped away from the garden, closing the door and walking over towards where the stables were. Both Aramis and Louie poked their heads out when they saw him coming and Louie shouted loudly.

"I think they're hungry. Perhaps we should feed the boys first?" he said. "Come on, this way. Hold on boys."

Grandad stepped around the side of the stables with Ciara and Maddy behind him. Ciara was surprised to find a little wooden barn had been built on the back of the stone structure. Grandad opened a door in it and ushered them inside.

"This is the feed room," he said.

Ciara looked around herself at the array of bins, each labelled in white paint. One said simply Chicken.

"Grab them buckets Ciara," Grandad said pointing to two black rubber buckets by the door. "Maddy, you lift the lid on that bin, there should be a scoop inside."

Maddy found the blue scoop and held it up for Grandad to see, he nodded. "Right, Ciara, take the scoop and fill it once from each bin and put it into the buckets. Then take that spoon hanging on the hook and mix it around. Throw some water in from the jug too, that's it." Ciara did as she was asked and filled the buckets. "Now then, let's pop their feeds in. Me and Maddy will take Louie's, you take Aramis's, you remember how to ask him to step back."

Ciara swallowed and nodded. She'd never fed any of the horses before, Fairbanks didn't really have anyone do any stable work unless they were a teenager. She picked up the bucket and followed Grandad around to the stables. Louie shouted and stamped his foot, but Aramis stood patiently.

With a deep breath, Ciara unbolted the door. "Back," she said and Aramis took a step back, she entered the stable and placed the bucket down on the floor. Seconds later Aramis's nose disappeared in the bucket and the sound of happy munching filled the air.

"Well, that'll keep them busy for a few minutes, we'll feed the others then turn them out," Grandad said.

"Chickens!" Maddy said, jumping a little.

They gathered the feed for the sheep, goats, and chickens from the little feed room and went around passing it out. The sheep were a little standoffish and Ciara wasn't too fond of the chickens, though Maddy loved them, the two little goats were friendly, though they nibbled at Ciara's pocket.

"We can collect the eggs later," Grandad said to Maddy as opened up the door on the chicken coop and tossed a little extra corn on the grass floor of their outdoor run. Maddy smiled. "First though we turn out the horses and have a nice cup of tea. You want to help me turn out Ciara?"

Ciara smiled nervously. "Me? I mean, yes, but I haven't done it before."

Grandad frowned. "Never, not even at riding school?"

Ciara shook her head. "We lead to the mounting block a few times."

"Well, time you learnt then, and how to muck out too!" Grandad said. "Fancy, teaching to ride but not stable management. Maddy, you go on back inside, see if your Mum's up yet and if she fancy's putting the kettle on."

"Ok," Maddy grinned.

"Ciara, you grab that green headcollar from the peg on the feed room door." Ciara nodded and lifted the headcollar off the door while Grandad took down a red one.

Quietly they walked back to the stables and Grandad nodded his head in the direction of Aramis. "You get him, he's good on the lead rope, I'll get Louie."

Ciara looked at the head collar and up at Aramis. "I don't think I can reach."

Grandad laughed. "Here, tell you what, let's turn Aramis out first, then Louie, together." Ciara smiled. Grandad guided her over to Aramis's door and opened it. He handed her a little piece of carrot from his pocket. "Ok, I want you to click at him and then say down, point your finger down too. He'll lower his head, then you can slip on the head collar and give him the carrot."

"Really?" Ciara asked.

"Try it."

Ciara followed Grandad's instructions and sure enough, Aramis lowered his head and stood quietly while she put the head collar on.

"That's amazing!" Ciara said.

Grandad laughed. "That's training. Louie isn't quite there yet though. Ok, take the lead rope in both hands, that's it, and you're going to look where you are going, keep your shoulders relaxed, if you tense, he'll tense, it's just the same as when you ride. Now, start walking towards that gate opposite us."

Ciara did what Grandad said and Aramis dutifully followed her towards the gate. Grandad walked beside her and when they reached the field he opened the gate so they could walk in.

"Turn him around to face the gate, that's it. Now, ask him to come down again and take off the headcollar."

"Down," Ciara said and smiled as Aramis lowered his head and she could undo the headcollar buckle.

Aramis walked away from them a little way, dropped into the dust by the gate, and rolled happily.

"Thanks for that," Grandad said in his direction. Ciara laughed.

"Right, let's go get the thug," Grandad smirked. Ciara glanced at him. "Oh, don't get me wrong, I love Louie but he's like a bull in a china shop compared to Aramis."

"Did they come from the same place?" Ciara asked as they crossed back to Louie who was nudging the door impatiently.

Grandad shook his head. "Aramis belonged to a friend of mine, Davey Pearce," Grandad said as he slipped a headcollar on Louie. "You get the gate this time Ciara." She nodded and they set off towards the field, Louie jogging a little by Grandad's shoulder. "Walk," he said and grudgingly Louie walked. Ciara opened the gate and Grandad set Louie free to trot around and roll.

"What was I saying, oh, yes, Aramis. Davey brought him to replace his older horse, Piper, we both used to do demonstrations at the museum, showing how horses used to plough and such like. After I lost Max it was down to Davey, but with Piper getting on he decided to start a youngster."

"How did you end up with him?" Ciara asked.

"Ah, well, last year Davey had a stroke, he's ok, but his arm's weak now, he can't handle training a youngster and he couldn't bear to see Aramis go to some stranger. He knew I was looking again and here we are. I promised to take Piper up for the displays this year and train Aramis on to take over, for as long as I can manage it that is."

"And Louie?" Ciara asked, watching the young horse as he leapt off all four feet.

Grandad shook his head. "Got him from a friend of a friend, stud owner that breeds ride and drives and Connemara ponies." At that last word Ciara froze, her mind suddenly filled with Misty. Grandad nodded. "You Mum said you used to ride a Connie. Special, was she?"

Ciara swallowed the lump that had formed in her throat and nodded. "Misty," she said. "She's called Misty."

Grandad pulled her into a hug. "Big change this for all of you isn't it." She hung her head, not sure what to say. "Tell you what though, I'm glad you're here. Say, why don't we have that cup of tea and I'll show you how to muck out and you can tell me all about this pony."

Ciara smiled and nodded.

Chapter 6

"Now, just sift the shavings a little and see, the muck will fall out and you can scoop it up into the wheelbarrow," Grandad said with a smile as he emptied his shaving fork into the blue barrow parked by the door. Ciara smiled back amazed at how simple it was, she couldn't believe they hadn't taught them this at riding school.

"Grab that shovel, will you?" Grandad said, pointing to an old, wooden-handled shovel he had balanced by the door. Ciara picked it up and handed it to Grandad, it weighed a ton and she wondered at how easily Grandad lifted it. "Right now, I'll load up all the wet we found, you have a go with the fork, see if you can find any poo we missed." he smiled.

Ciara began to try and lift the shavings, shifting them as she went. While it had looked easy, it took Ciara a few goes before she could keep the fork head straight. Soon enough though, she was happily helping Grandad fill the barrow, tossing the shavings up to the walls of the stable and sifting through them. When they were done, Grandad showed her how to pull the bed back down and pat it flat so it was comfortable for Louie to sleep on.

"Shall we do Aramis now? He's cleaner than Louie," he said with a smile. Ciara nodded and smiled back. "Come on then. After that maybe we can get Aramis to work for his supper, eh?"

Ciara smiled and picked up the fork. "Do you muck out everything every day?" she asked.

"Sure do," Grandad said. "Sometimes, if it's really bad weather I might leave the wet in for a night, but it's rare. Better to have them all fluffed up and soft I think. When we're done we'll empty this in the compost heap too, then we'll have some brilliant compost for the garden in a few months. Don't tell your sister though, I'm not sure she'd appreciate where the compost I'll give her for the flowers came from," he smirked.

"Promise." Ciara laughed imagining the look on Maddy's face if she found out.

Ciara began to push the shavings to the side of the stable walls in Aramis's stable while Grandad did the same with the shovel. She couldn't help but notice that the stables were freshly painted and bright.

"What are you going to do with Aramis today?" Ciara asked.

"I think we'll get him on the long lines," Grandad said, throwing wet shavings into the wheelbarrow.

"What are they?" Ciara asked with a frown.

"Did you ever do groundwork at riding school?" Grandad asked. Ciara shook her head. "Well, I'll show you, come on, this looks pretty clean now. You take the tools back to the shed and I'll empty the barrow."

A few minutes later, Ciara watched as Grandad led Aramis out of the field and tied him up to a ring on the fence close to the paddock. He waved Ciara over and she walked up, realising once again just how much bigger Aramis was than Misty. Thinking of the little bay pony made her falter a little. She'd usually be riding her about now. Ciara wondered if she was being used in a lesson at that second or if some other kid was riding her around the arena. Was she happy, did she wonder where Ciara was?

Grandad glanced at her as he put a box down on the little wooden mounting block that stood by the fence and popped it open revealing a series of brushes.

"You have brushed before," he said rather than asked and Ciara nodded trying not to look glum. It was the one thing she had done, but only on Misty. She picked up a brush and curry comb and began to brush Aramis's coat as high as she could while trying to pull her thoughts from Misty. Grandad laughed and shook his head as he watched her try to stand on tip-toe to reach Aramis's back.

"Here." He picked up the box and put it on the ground before pulling the mounting block up beside Aramis. The grey vaguely looked at it but then swished a fly away with his tail and went back to dozing in the sunshine.

Ciara climbed on the box and began brushing his back, it was much easier with the block to stand on. Aramis's withers twitched as she drew the brush over the area and she paused, taking the brush away. "I'm not sure he likes that bit being done," she said, looking over at Grandad.

"Look at his face and ears," Grandad said. "His back leg. The ears are flopped to the side, his leg is resting, his head is low, and he's totally relaxed. Look, even his lower lip has dropped open a bit. No, it's not that he doesn't like it, it's just a bit tickly. Try scratching there, really give him a good scratch and watch what he does."

Ciara frowned, she put the brush down and began to scratch at Aramis's withers. His head raised a little and he tilted it slightly, moving his shoulder just a little so that she was scratching just to the left of where she had been before and then he began to wiggle his lips. At first, his top lip waved back and forth, then he made a few little nibbly actions as if he was imagining he was grooming another horse. Ciara laughed at him as he pulled funny faces and leaned closer to her.

"See, itchy spot," Grandad said. "He's terrible for it really, he'd stand there all day and let you scratch him."

They finished brushing and Grandad brought out a bridle, a roller with lots of different rings on it, and two very long ropes with lead rope clips on the end. He smiled and hung them on the fence.

"Right, let's get started. This is the roller, we'll pop this on first." Very gently Grandad lifted the roller off the fence and placed it over Aramis's back so it sat where a saddle would. "It's like a big girth that goes all the way around him," Grandad said. "We fasten it with these two buckles here." He did up the straps and checked it was tight enough.

"Ok, grab the bridle," Grandad said. Ciara went to get it and handed it to Grandad. "Thank you. Have you tacked up yourself?"

Ciara shook her head. "I watched a lot, but no one ever said what they were doing or anything."

Grandad nodded. "Ok, now, we pop the bridle in one hand, the other hand goes under the bit like this and we put the hand with the bridle over his nose and then present the bit under his mouth." Aramis happily opened his mouth and took the bit, chomping on it a little. "And then the headpiece goes over his ears, there we go, bridle on. Just need to fasten the noseband and throat lash, come on, you have a go with the noseband."

Ciara helped fasten the little buckle at the bottom of the noseband. "There are no reins," Ciara noticed.

"Because we'll use them," Grandad said, pointing to the ropes. He picked them up and attached one to each of the rings of the bit and then threaded them through the rings at the side of the roller. Tossing the ropes behind Aramis, Grandad walked to the rear of him and picked them up. "See, now I can direct him just as if I were riding without being on top. It helps when he learns to drive and for when he's backed. Open the gate up will you?"

Ciara opened the gate to the paddock next to the one Louie was grazing in and Grandad clicked his tongue and gently tapped Aramis on the flank with one of the ropes. "Walk on."

Aramis walked into the paddock and Grandad began to get the big horse to work around him in a large circle using the ropes and his voice to guide him. "We want him to look in towards me and use the ropes to help to ask him to do that. The outside rope we use to move him on, little taps on his hindquarters to say speed up and little squeezes to say slow down. Inside tells him to look in."

Ciara nodded. "What about turns? How do you ask him to change direction?"

"Well, then we open the outside rope, we ask him to change direction and we tap with the inside one." Grandad changed direction as he spoke, showing her how it was done. Ciara stood fascinated by the fence. "Trot."

Aramis began to trot around Grandad happily for a few circles. Ciara lent on the fence watching and was soon joined by Louie who stood with his head over the fence next to her. "You're going to do that soon," she said to him. Louie snorted and Ciara giggled.

"Ciara come on here," Grandad said. She joined Grandad and he put the ropes in her hands, keeping his own on them too. "Nice and gentle, that's it. Now he's slowing down, give him just a little tap and say walk on."

Nervously Ciara did as she was told and Aramis picked his pace up just a little, making her smile.

They did a few more minutes on both reins before Grandad had Aramis stop and took off both the roller and one of the ropes, hanging them on the fence.

"Is he finished?" Ciara asked.

"Pretty much, I like to keep it short especially if he's tried hard, but we always end with some in-hand work."

"What's that?" Ciara asked.

"We're going to play follow my leader," he smiled.

Ciara looked confused and Grandad smiled at her. He began to walk away from Aramis, letting out a little of the rope as he went, Aramis ambled along behind him, following Grandad as he moved in circles or turned left or right. It seemed like the horse watched his every move, ready to follow his lead. Ciara thought it was amazing, she wondered if Misty would have followed her like that if they had tried it. Grandad stopped and held up a hand and Aramis stopped. Grandad turned around to face him.

"Back," he said and Aramis stepped back. "Good lad.

"Down," Grandad pointed his finger down and Aramis lowered his head. Grandad patted him and handed over a little piece of carrot.

"How do you do that?" Ciara asked, amazed.

Grandad chuckled. "Patience, kindness and practise. Eventually we'll do this without the rope, just loose." He passed the rope to Ciara. "Ok, you walk, if he gets too close to you, turn away, and make him follow you. If he gets really close, wave the rope a little at him. This is about your space and his. We want to be kind, but in charge."

Ciara nodded and began leading Aramis around. For the most part, he did just as he had with Grandad, though once or twice Grandad told her he was too close, and to ask him back off.

"Good job," Grandad said after a few minutes. Ciara beamed. "Now if you can get him to do that," Grandad chuckled, pointing at Louie with his thumb, "I'd be seriously impressed."

"He doesn't do this?" Ciara asked.

"He does, but he's just starting really. Learning," Grandad said.

"Grandad!" Maddy called running down towards the field. "Mum said she's too busy to go down to see the sea."

"Oh, go on then. We'll put Aramis back out and pop down for a minute. Go ask your brother if he wants to come."

Maddy shook her head, her pigtails flying. "Branden just got up, he's having breakfast."

"That boy needs something to do," Grandad said with a thoughtful smile. "Would you grab the rope and roller Ciara, I'll pop Aramis out." Ciara nodded.

Aramis rolled again as soon as he was loose and Grandad shook his head with a glance at the grooming kit, Ciara just giggled.

"Beach!" Maddy bounced.

Grandad took her hand and together they headed down the driveway. It only took a few minutes to reach the gate with the peeling paint. Ciara looked at it thoughtfully.

"The gate looks a little drab," she said.

Grandad nodded as they checked for cars and crossed the road. "I know, a lot of the house does, but when there's only you there, I don't know, it seems a little pointless to get painting. Besides, I have a lot of things to get done, so as long as it's clean I'm ok."

"It's not just you now though," Maddy said as they stepped into the dunes. Grandad looked down at her with a smile.

They climbed through the rolling dunes, weaving between the coarse grasses, and soon emerged onto the beach. Ciara stood and stared. They were stood on a wide curving stretch of flat beach, the soft sand slowly turning firm as it reached the waves that lapped onto the shore with fluffy, foamy tops. Far off at the end of the arched beach was a jutting hulk of dark stone where the waves crashed much more intensely. It was beautiful and wild.

"Wow!" Maddy said. "I'm putting my feet in the sea!" she said, stripping off her socks and shoes.

"Whoa there," Grandad said. "Hold on. Now, you can walk up to your ankles all the way along, but if you ever go swimming you have to stay in the middle of the curve. That far end, with the rock, the waves there are always too big to swim and there's a rip current at the other side. Understand?"

They nodded. "Ok, ankle deep only." Maddy nodded and skipped off towards the water. Grandad picked up her shoes and socks with a smile and started walking after her, Ciara beside him. She never really liked going in the sea unless it was really hot, and while the early summer sunshine was nice, it wasn't that hot.

"So, this pony from the riding school, what did you say she was called," Grandad asked, not taking his eyes off Maddy who was jumping over the little waves squealing.

"Misty," Ciara said, feeling a pang of sorrow.

"And she's a Connie, yes?"

"Yeah," Ciara nodded. "She's bay, and perfect."

Grandad smiled. "Perfect?"

Ciara nodded. "I don't know, it's like we just..."

"Fit," Grandad said with a knowing nod. "You know Connemara's were originally bay."

"Really?" Ciara said. "I thought they were grey?"

Grandad smiled. "There are a lot of greys now, but that's because the breed has a lot of Iberian horse blood in it now. A long time ago Spanish horses washed ashore and bred with them, now there are a lot of greys."

"Really?" Ciara asked.

Grandad nodded. "Some ships even washed up here, but they were mostly smugglers, and a few pirates," he smiled.

"Pirates!" Ciara said, her eyes going wide.

"Well, that's what they say. Not sure I believe it." He chuckled.

Ciara thought for a moment. As much as she wanted to know the pirate story, something else had been playing on her mind, and standing on the wide-open beach seemed like the perfect time to ask.

"Grandad, the trophy, the one in the living room. It's yours, right?"

Grandad nodded. "Yeah, that's mine. Well, mine and Max's. It was the last show held at the big house. What a sight that was, competing on the big show field." Grandad smiled.

"They don't hold it anymore?" Ciara asked.

Grandad took a deep breath. "Well, actually, this year I hear they held a smaller version, mostly kids games, a few ridden classes. Oh, but in the day, there were in-hand classes, and driving, it was something to see. And the house, oh, it's lovely."

"You went in?" Ciara asked.

Grandad smiled. "Sure did, you see the lady in the picture presenting the trophy?"

Ciara thought hard, she remembered the trophy, but not a picture with a lady in it. She shook her head.

"Well, when we get back maybe I can pull out the old picture album, and we can take a look." He smiled. "I'll show you Mrs. Fitz and the manor. You know it's close to the riding school I was talking about before. I wish I could remember its name."

"Oh, oh, it's freezing," Maddy said, running up to them and hopping about. "The water's soo cold."

Ciara giggled as Grandad handed Maddy her socks, she looked at them and her face fell as she realised her socks were going to get sandy.

"Maybe I should have brought Aramis with us," Grandad mused. "He could have carried you back."

Chapter 7

"There you go," Grandad said, handing Ciara, Maddy, and Branden mugs of warm tea. "Perfect for cold toes that have dipped in the sea."

Maddy giggled and wiggled her toes as she took a sip from the brown stoneware mug. Ciara smiled and turned the page in the photo album she had balanced on her knee. They had gathered in the living room when they had got home and Grandad had pulled out a ton of old albums. Some had pictures of Mum as a little girl, others had photos of Grandad with his horses. Ciara smiled as she flipped through, she paused looking at one image. It showed Grandad standing beside Max, his bridle covered in ribbons, while a smartly dressed lady in a tweed jacket handed him the trophy that stood on the sideboard.

"This was when you won?" she said, glancing up at Grandad while he settled down into his chair.

"Sure was," he smiled.

"Hey, look at this one of Mum," Branden laughed, spinning an album around to show them a picture of Mum standing in the living room in a big frilly powder blue dress. Ciara laughed and looked up as Mum came in.

"Oh, Dad! Did you need to show them this?" She took hold of the album and smiled. "This was cousin Susie's wedding."

Grandad smiled. Maddy popped her head up and glanced at the picture then frowned. "It looks the same."

"What does sweetie?" Mum asked, hugging her.

"The living room," Maddy said.

Ciara looked around, Maddy was right, it was exactly the same as in the picture, only Mum looked a lot younger. Grandad sighed.

"I guess it could do with a tidy-up." He said. "Hey, maybe since you're here you could help me spruce this place up a little."

"YES!" Mum yelled, then she burst out laughing as did Ciara.

"Well, I'm glad you're keen," Grandad chuckled. "Maybe Branden here could help you."

Branden looked up from the photo album in his hands and raised his eyebrow. "Me?"

"Why not?" Grandad said. "As far as I remember you know how to use a paintbrush."

Branden opened his mouth then shrugged. "I guess I don't have band practice to go to."

"About that," Grandad said. "While we're on digging out the decorating gear from the garage, maybe we could tidy it up a bit, and give you somewhere to go practice."

"Cool," Branden nodded. Ciara smiled.

Mum jumped a little and fumbled in her pocket, pulling out her buzzing phone. "It's Dad," she said, hitting the answer button. "Mitch? Hey, how's it going, hold on I'll put you on speaker."

Mum pressed a button on her phone and held it out. "Hi, we're all here," she said.

"Hey, guys," Dad's voice filtered through the phone. "How's it going at Grandad's?"

"I went in the sea!" Maddy shouted. "It was cold."

Ciara giggled. "Sorry I missed it," Dad said. "How about you Branden, you doing ok."

"I guess," Branden said a little flatly.

"Ciara?"

"I'm ok, I helped Grandad with Aramis and Louie," she said.

"Who are Aramis and Louie?" Dad asked.

"My new draughts," Grandad said. "She's a great little helper with the horses."

"Maybe we can find another riding school close by then," Dad said. Ciara could hear him smiling, but she felt her own smile fade.

"I don't know," she said. "Another school won't have Misty. Maybe I can just help Grandad with Aramis and Louie."

Things went quiet. Mum hugged her and smiled. "How's work going?" she asked Dad.

"Can't complain, but I miss you all. It's very strange coming back from work to an empty hotel room," Dad said.

"Kinda strange for us too," Branden pointed out.

Ciara swallowed hard. The fun of earlier seemed to be fading away. For a few hours, learning about the horses Ciara had felt almost happy. Maddy had laughed on the beach and smiled. Even Branden had lit up just a little at the idea of having a place to play his music. Now though, everyone looked a little gloomy again.

"I know," Dad's voice said. "I know."

Mum smiled at everyone and shrugged a little, pushing a button on the phone and putting it back to her ear. "I'm just going to talk to Dad for a while ok?"

"Sure," Grandad said with a nod. "We'll go down to town, and get some paint."

Mum raised her eyebrow, but Branden had already thrown himself out of the chair and run towards the door. "Shotgun!"

"Hey, no fair," Ciara yelled, chasing after him.

*

Ciara hadn't known what to expect from 'town', but it wasn't the small assemblage of shops they pulled up outside of. At home, there had been shops around every corner, streets of glass-fronted stores with everything from clothes and shoes to fine wines and wallpaper. Grandad's town was a series of five or six stores lined up along one side of the road facing out over a little harbour. Several houses were clustered behind them, as was a large hotel that looked as though it had once been very grand, but had faded a little.

"Here we go," Grandad said, pulling up his old estate car and unbuckling his belt.

Ciara looked along the series of shops. One had an assortment of buckets, spades, and fishing nets hung outside.

"That there," Grandad said, pointing to a little shop with blue window frames and a neon sign in the window. "That's the chippy, we can pick up fish and chips for tea. Best for miles."

"Eak!" Maddy squealed happily.

"What else is there?" Branden asked.

"Ah, well there's the ice cream parlour, Sykes place."

"There's ice cream!" Maddy beamed.

"Yeah, but it's closed. Derek and Joyce who own it, they go on holiday for the last two weeks of term, so they're back for the summer holidays starting up. We get a few tourists you know. Anyway, this year their trip was put back a few days, they'll be open next weekend." Grandad said. "We'll come back then, eh?" Maddy nodded. "That's Louise's, Aladdin's Cave, artsy place, does crystals and art and that sort of thing," Grandad said pointing to another shop on the front with huge geode's in the window. "There's the pharmacy and John's place, that's where we're headed."

Grandad pointed to a large double-fronted store with an assortment of buckets and spades hung outside. They stepped out of the car and headed toward the shops. The smell of fish and chips hit Ciara, along with the hint of the sea.

"Can we see the harbour too?" Ciara asked.

"Sure," Grandad said. He locked the car and led them down the street of shops, over the road, and past a couple of houses to the large harbour wall. They stood together looking out over the bobbing boats nestled together.

"Look," Maddy said, pointing to a little boat just pulling in.

"Ah, that'll be the tour boat," Grandad said. "It takes folks out to look for seals and other wildlife."

"What's that?" Branden asked as he nodded to a sign on a stand by the harbour. Ciara looked to see a picture of a horse pulling a cart full of fish up from the harbour next to some test.

"Oh, that's how they used to get the fish up to the markets," Grandad said with a smile. "Come on, we need paint."

Grandad led them back up the street and into the store with the buckets and spade's outside. One side of the shop seemed to be filled with decorating materials and gardening supplies, while the other focused on souvenirs, toys, and gifts. A boy about Brandon's age was stacking paint can's up on a shelf when they came in. He smiled at them and swept long dirty blond hair from his face.

"Hey, Mr. Ross, you want my Dad?" he asked.

"No, that's alright Luke, we just need some paint." Grandad ushered them towards the paint swatches and then paused. "Say, Luke, you met my grandson?"

"Er, no," Luke said.

Grandad waved Branden over, "Hey Branden, this is Luke, he'll be in the same school year as you."

"What's up?" Luke asked, smiling at Branden, he frowned a little and waved a hand at Branden's belt buckle. "Hey, you like the Raven?"

"Yeah," Branden smiled. "I saw them last year."

"No way!" Luke said. "Oh, you gotta tell me what it was like!"

The two wandered off together and Grandad chuckled. "Let's look at the paint." He smiled at Ciara and Maddy.

*

Two hours later Ciara sat at the kitchen table picking at the few chips left on her paper. Grandad was right, they were the best fish and chips she had ever had. Even Maddy had cleared her portion. Mum lent back in her chair.

"Oh, my," she said around a mouthful of fish. "I forgot how awesome these are."

Grandad smiled. "We got paint too. Some for the living room, some for in here."

"We even got some to paint the dark wardrobe in our room," Maddy added with a smile. Mum smiled too and mouthed a thank you at Grandad. He just grinned.

Ciara looked around wondering what it would look like all painted freshly. A new start, Grandad had said, she guessed it couldn't hurt. Maybe if they all chipped in it would feel a little more like home and maybe, just maybe, it would take her mind off Misty.

"Well," Grandad pushed himself away from the table. "I had best get the rest of the chores done. Looks like we might get a bit of a storm."

Ciara looked out of the window at the dark clouds gathering. Maddy hated storms, Ciara looked over at her and saw her face full of worry.

"Hey, you want to play a game?" she asked. Maddy nodded. "Branden?"

"Sure," he grinned.

Mum smiled, "I'll sort out this then," she said waving at the table.

"Ok, but Ciara, pop out in ten minute ok, I could do with a hand getting the boys in and fed before it rains."

Ciara nodded and headed into the living room following Maddy and Branden. They settled down on the rug, while Branden opened the cupboard in the sideboard and started telling them the games they could play. Most of them were for grown-ups and they ended up playing snap.

They had played a few rounds before it grew so dark that Branden put the light on. Ciara frowned. "I think I'll go help Grandad, it's looking really dark."

"Go on," Branden said. "I'll play with Mad's, maybe I'll win."

"No way!" Maddy said with a little smile.

Ciara stood up and headed to the boot room. Mum had finished cleaning up the papers and was wiping down the surfaces with a cloth, she smiled as Ciara headed to get her boots.

Outside it felt warm but with a hint of something in the air that told Ciara it was more than rain coming. She looked down towards the sea, above the dunes, she could see the sky had turned almost navy blue. It was definitely time to be inside.

She walked towards the stables but couldn't see Grandad. Aramis and Louie were stood by the gate patiently. It surprised Ciara that Grandad hadn't got them in already.

"Grandad?" she called heading around to the feed room. "Grandad?"

"Ciara!" she heard Grandad call urgently.

Ciara ran around the end of the stables towards the feed room. Grandad was laid on the floor by the door.

"Grandad!" She rushed over to try and help him up, but he didn't move.

"I slipped, hurt my back," Grandad said, wincing. "Go get your Mum."

Ciara rushed back to the house, her feet pounding across the driveway. She burst through the door calling for Mum and Branden, her heart pounding. The next few minutes were a blur. Mum flew out of the door, Branden behind her. Ciara took Maddy's hand and they ran too. Mum helped Grandad up, but it was obvious he had done something serious. Mum looked worried. She ran to pull the car up by the stables and with Branden's help, got Grandad into the back of it.

"Just get me inside Laura," he protested, but Mum shook her head.

"I'm taking you to the hospital, Branden you're in charge," she said sliding into the driver's seat.

Branden closed the door behind her and then stood back next to Ciara and Maddy as Mum pulled away in a shower of stones. Ciara looked up at Branden.

"Ok, ok," Branden said. "It's fine, it's going to be fine. Erm, we just, we just need to," he looked around confused. "What do we need to do?"

"Get Louie and Aramis in," Ciara said "And the chickens and goats."

"Ok, you get the horses, I'll go with Maddy and do the chickens and goats," Branden said.

"And the sheep." Maddy nodded. "Before..." She trailed off looking at the storm clouds.

"Let's go," Branden said.

Ciara took a deep breath and looked over at Aramis and Louie. She took Louie's headcollar off his door and crossed over to the field.

"I can do this, I can do this," she said to herself. "Ok, Louie, here we go." She clicked her tongue "Down." She pointed her finger and to her surprise, he lowered his head just a little. Ciara smiled and slid his headcollar on.

"Back," she said. Louie looked at her. She rattled the lead rope a little. "Back." She tried again with a little more energy. This time Louie shuffled back enough for Ciara to open the gate. He walked out and turned around as she closed the gate.

"I'll be right back," she said to Aramis, and led Louie across to his stable. Once he was inside she had him lower his head again and took the headcollar off.

"One down," she said as she closed the door and headed back to Aramis.

Aramis, always the gentlemen, did exactly as Ciara asked and in no time she had him in his stable. Thankfully she remembered that she and Grandad had filled their hay racks that morning, so she wouldn't have to work out how to get the hay up into them.

"Feed," she said to herself.

Closing Aramis's door, she headed around to the feed room. The clouds which had been out at sea were now rapidly approaching. Branden and Maddy were shutting up the little shed the goats slept in and Ciara noticed the chickens and sheep were already inside.

"You done?" Branden called as the first rattle of thunder boomed. Maddy jumped and grabbed his hand.

"Just have to feed them," Ciara said.

"Ok," Branden said. "Let's sort it together, ok?"

Ciara thought back to what Grandad had told her Aramis and Louie ate. She filled their buckets and with her carrying one bucket and Maddy the other, they headed back to the stables while Branden bolted up the feed room.

Ciara unbolted the doors and put the boy's feeds in before bolting them again. A flash of lightning lit up the sky making Maddy jump and clutch Ciara's arm.

"Come on," Branden said rounding the corner. "Inside, now."

He ushered them inside as the rain began to fall and the thunder boomed. Ciara glanced out of the window at the storm hoping Grandad was ok. Branden put his hand on her shoulder.

"It'll be ok," he said. "Right now, I think Maddy needs us most." Ciara nodded, looking out one last time as a flash of lightning lit up the dunes.

Chapter 8

Ciara stirred at the sound of the front door being unlocked. As she sat up a thick blanket, usually draped on the back of the sofa, slid off her. She realised she'd fallen asleep on the couch with Maddy, Branden must have put the blanket over them. The sound of the front door opening made her sit up further, sliding out of the blanket being careful not to wake Maddy.

Branden stood up from the chair by the fire and put his finger to his lips, before leading the way into the hall. Mum jumped when they stepped out into the passage.

"Maddy's asleep on the sofa," Branden said in a whisper. "How's Grandad?"

Mum pointed to the kitchen and the three of them quietly walked down the hallway together. As soon as they were in the kitchen, Mum made her way to the stove and put the kettle on. Ciara sat down at the table, while Branden lent against the little bit of work surface that surrounded the sink under the window.

"Grandad's ok," Mum said, pulling three mugs out of a cupboard. "We were in A&E for ages before we were seen. They think he's just bruised, but they want to do a few x-rays to make sure so they're keeping him in overnight. Well, for the few hours of it that are left."

"That's a relief," Branden said. Mum nodded.

"You should really get a few hours more sleep," Mum said, pouring out some tea.

"I'm not sure I can," Branden said sitting down opposite Ciara.

"Me either," she shook her head.

"Best try, looks like we might have to take care of things for a while," Mum smiled. "Look, why don't we all just have a camp out together in the living room, like we used to when you were little."

Branden and Ciara looked at each other and then nodded. "I'll go get blankets and pillows," Branden said.

Ciara did fall back asleep for a while, curled up on the couch on the opposite side to Maddy. The sun was up and streaming through the windows when she finally opened her eyes. Mum was asleep on the floor, wrapped in her duvet, but Branden wasn't in the chair, his blanket had been pushed aside. Ciara stood up and as she did Maddy stirred, she sat up and stretched her arms.

"Grandad?" she asked sleepily.

Mum groaned and sat up on the floor as Branden opened the door with a tray in his hands.

"Breakfast. I have toast, I have tea, I have a bowl of cocoa pops," Branden said, setting down the tray.

"Thank you," Mum said, sitting up and grabbing a mug from the tray and hovering over it.

"Branden is up?" Maddy said. Everyone giggled.

"Yeah, I think we all need to get up too," Mum said. "Those animals won't see to themselves."

"I can feed the chickens." Maddy beamed.

Mum nodded. "Well, I know how to handle the sheep and the goats."

"Really?" Branden asked.

Mum smiled and winked at him. "Ciara, you think you could see to the horses?"

Ciara nodded. "Sure, Grandad taught me how to do their stables."

They ate and Ciara stood up to get dressed just as the phone in the hall. Mum rushed over to it and picked it up.

"Yes, yes, yes that's fine. Ok, thank you," Mum said. She put the phone down. "Grandad is fine, I can pick him up in a few hours. The doctor says he needs to take it easy though, at least for a week. So, I guess for a week we're looking after all the animals. We'd best get going."

Branden opted to clean up the breakfast dishes while they headed outside. Ciara grabbed breakfast for Aramis and Louie, putting in their buckets before gathering the wheelbarrow and filling it with hay. Louie finished his food first and Ciara turned him out followed by Aramis, before using Grandad's pitch fork to lift the hay up into the hay rack. Remembering what Grandad had taught her, she mucked out each of their stables and filled their buckets. An hour later she stood proudly outside looking at her handiwork.

"Wow, good job," Mum said as she and Maddy came around from the chicken's hut.

"Thanks," Ciara said.

"Oh, look at the time, I need to wash up and go get Grandad."

They headed inside to find Branden standing in the hallway with a paintbrush in his hand. He smiled at them. "I figured I'd make a start. Don't touch the cupboard in your room ok," he said pointing the brush in the direction of Maddy and Ciara. They exchanged a look and then ran towards their room to see what Branden had done.

*

Mum helped Grandad out of the car and began to usher him towards the house, but he waved her off.

"I'm fine, I need to sort out the animals," Grandad said slowly making his way towards the stables. "Wait, who turned the boys out?"

"I did," Ciara said with a smile. "I mucked out too, just like you taught me."

"And I did the chickens!" Maddy said.

"Well now," Grandad said, poking his head over the door. "Isn't that something? Laura, couldn't fetch me a deck chair could you?"

"A deck chair?" Mum asked with a frown.

"Yep, there's one in the garage," Grandad said, waving a hand at it.

"Ok," Mum headed over to the garage and came back a few minutes later with a bright blue deck chair. "Where do you want it?"

"By the field," Grandad said. Mum smiled as she set it up beside the mounting block. "Perfect. Going to sit out and get some fresh air, stuffy in that hospital. Maybe Ciara can keep me company a bit."

"Ok," Mum said, she narrowed her eyes. "No doing anything mind."

Grandad just nodded and waved at her as she headed back into the house. Ciara walked over and sat on the mounting block watching Aramis and Louie.

"You did a good job with those beds," Grandad said "You have any trouble getting their headcollars on?"

"No, Louie even lowered his head," Ciara said.

Grandad nodded, he looked at her and smiled. "I wonder. I was thinking I'd have to put training on hold while these bruises heal, but maybe not, maybe you could do it?"

"Me?" Ciara asked.

"Why not?" Grandad said with a smile. "I can tell you what to do, you can be my hands. We'll leave Louie, apart from the headcollar bits, but I reckon you could long line Aramis with a bit of help."

Ciara suddenly felt unsure. It was one thing to lead Louie and Aramis, quite another to work with them. She swallowed hard.

"Let's start small," Grandad said. "You get the grooming kit, bring him in, and we'll brush him."

Ciara bit her lip. "Ok," she smiled. She fetched the box and headcollar, caught Aramis, and brought him to the fence, following Grandad's instructions. He stood patiently while she moved the mounting block closer and began to brush his coat.

"See, easy," Grandad said.

"Tell me a bit more about that pony," Grandad said, sitting back in his chair. "What's she like, typical easy-going riding school pony is she?"

Ciara laughed out loud and shook her head as she swapped one brush for another. "Misty was anything but a typical riding school pony."

"How so?" Grandad said.

Ciara smiled as she began to brush Aramis's mane. "Well, for a start she was sort of bought by accident. Mrs. Barron, she went to the sales to get a big horse for the stables, something quiet, but she saw Misty trotting around and pulling faces at people, she just said she couldn't leave her there."

"Pulling faces?" Grandad asked.

"She likes to stick her tongue out," Ciara giggled thinking about how Misty would poke her head over the door with her pink tongue hanging out the side of her mouth.

"But you liked to ride her," Grandad said.

"More than anything," Ciara sighed. "She was so quick. Lots of the girls didn't like to ride her, they said she was too quirky, and she threw a couple of people."

"But not you?" Grandad asked.

Ciara shook her head. "No, she was always fine with me." Grandad nodded. "How's the grooming going?"

Ciara smiled as she realised the whole time she'd been talking to Grandad she'd been grooming Aramis with no issues at all. Talking about Misty had made her relax and she'd just done it. She patted Aramis.

"Misty wasn't naughty with the other girls though," Ciara said suddenly thinking Grandad might have the wrong impression of her. "She's just, I don't know, she doesn't like it if the rider is heavy-handed or a little rough."

"No horse does," said Grandad with a smile. "How is she with scary things, you think she'd like it here, with the waves? Maybe she can come on holidays," he laughed.

"I think she'd like that," Ciara giggled. "She's not a spooky horse, we did a fancy dress at the little school show last year and I wore a dress, she didn't even bother when I sat on her in it."

"Well, that's good," Grandad said. "Never did fancy dress myself. Might have made a good cowboy though."

Ciara laughed and looked at Aramis. "Maybe the next show?" she suggested.

Grandad laughed. "Be more scarecrow than cowboy," he said. "Should we pop Aramis back out for a bit?" Grandad asked.

Ciara nodded and turned Aramis back out with Louie. She felt proud of herself and Grandad smiled.

"You know," Grandad said. "It's a shame I don't have someone that could be a steady companion to ride Louie with. Can't ride Aramis and him at the same time and I tell you what, Louie isn't too sure about the waves."

"Really?" Ciara said looking over at Louie who flicked his ears back and forth.

Grandad lowered his voice conspiratorially. "He wouldn't put his foot in the last time we went down for a walk. Just stood staring at it and snorting, his eyes nearly popped out of his head." Grandad smiled and Ciara giggled, she could just imagine the enormous Louie looking scared of the wave, like a lion afraid of a mouse.

They continued chatting about Misty as they slowly headed back inside. Ciara volunteered to get the horses in later so that Grandad could sit down and relax for a while, but when they got inside they realised it might be easier said than done. Branden had covered a lot of things with old sheets from the garage and started painting in the hallway. It did look a lot brighter and nicer, the dust sheets aside.

"What do you think?" Branden said from atop a little ladder as they came in.

"Well, the sheets are a little much," Grandad said, "But otherwise I think you're doing a great job, just, let's leave the living room til I'm a bit more mobile, ok?"

"Ok," Branden smiled. "Sorry, it's just, I em, I'm not good with the animal stuff, well, at least I'm not as helpful, I don't know what to do with them. I can do this."

Grandad smiled. "You keep going then."

Branden beamed. "Ok," he nodded. "Hey, Ciara, can you pass me that tape?" He pointed to a roll of masking tape sitting on the stairs and she went to grab it as Grandad headed into the living room where Mum was waiting for him.

"You got good kids there Laura," Ciara heard him say. "Branden stepping up, decorating, Maddy with the sheep and chickens, she's just like you and Ciara, she's a very responsible young lady, taking care of my boys." Ciara smiled to herself.

Over the next week, Grandad taught her how to put the bridle and roller on Aramis and how to get him to move on the long lines. At first, she found the two long ropes a bit of a tangle, but soon enough she learnt how to sort them out and how to get Aramis to walk around on them. For the first few times, she walked slightly behind and to the side, but gradually Grandad talked her through getting him to walk around her, so she could stay almost still. She got him to change direction and back up before Grandad had her trot him too.

Every evening, when they sat in the lounge, Grandad would tell her how to improve and what they could try next. The days sped by and every day he asked her more and more stories about Misty while telling her his adventures with Max and teaching her how to work Aramis and, to a smaller extent Louie. One day he even had her bring out a few of Branden's dust sheets, weigh them down and walk Aramis over the top. Ciara had been worried he'd shy, but he followed her over it without a flinch and then even trotted over it. Working Aramis made her miss Misty more and at the same time made her feel happy and relaxed. She really enjoyed mucking them out too, her thoughts often drifted to the bay mare and she'd imagine she was mucking out her stable.

Branden was making changes too. Painting the wardrobe in Ciara and Maddy's room had made a huge difference, it seemed light and bright. Maddy had been super happy, especially when Branden had found a few old shelves in the garage he painted to match and put up for her stuffed animals to sit on. He painted the hallway in a nice sunny yellow so it was warm and light, before taking on the kitchen with Mum's help. It had transformed from a dark, old-fashioned space to one much more like the kitchen in their old house had been. He'd even promised Maddy he'd look at the garden with her and perhaps start sorting out the old play house. It had surprised Ciara that he knew what to do, but it turned out Grandad was helping

Branden with the decorating as much as he was Ciara with her horse knowledge.

One sunny evening, late in the week, Ciara sat drying her hair in her room looking out at the dusky sun. Louie was eating, but Aramis's head hung out of the stable watching the same sun-streaked sky she was. Down beyond the driveway, through the dunes, Ciara could just see the sea lapping against the soft sand. A chestnut horse and rider cantered along the sands and Ciara couldn't help but imagine what it would be like to have Misty here. Life would be perfect. The farm really was a nice place to be, it was looking much less drab now, she loved seeing the sea and being able to learn about horses every day. She liked working and looking after Aramis and Louie, they were just too big for her to safely ride. If only Misty were here too. If only she could canter along the sand with her, feel her hooves thudding along as they streamed past the sunset and the lapping waves. Ciara sighed. She wondered if she could ever get that perfect life.

Chapter 9

For a few days, Ciara enjoyed helping Grandad work with Louie and Aramis. Grandad kept saying how much help she was and how responsible. It made her feel happier than she had in a while. A week later, Grandad was much better and started doing a few things around the farm, even helping Branden finish decorating the lounge, which looked so much better painted in warm reds and yellows. Ciara couldn't help but think it would be amazingly cosy come the cooler weather, then she'd laughed at herself for thinking about it given that it was the beginning of summer.

Mum stepped into the kitchen and smiled. Branden had made everyone breakfast again and he was surprisingly good at bacon and eggs.

"Where's Grandad?" Maddy asked, grabbing another forkful of food.

"He's feeding the chickens," Mum said with a smile. "He says he's feeling better and he has an errand to run. He suggested we go down to the beach for the day."

"Really?" Maddy said with a smile.

Mum nodded. "I just checked the weather; it's going to be really hot. So, how about you all go and get ready and I pack us up a picnic."

Maddy launched herself out of her chair and ran for the door, followed by Ciara. Branden caught up to her in the corridor, catching her around the waist and swinging her around so that he was ahead of her on the stairs. Ciara laughed and swiped at his arm as she chased him upstairs.

It only took half an hour for them to be ready. Usually, it would take ages to be prepared for a beach trip, things would have to be packed in cars and even then, there would be a drive. At Grandad's though all it took was a picnic basket, a backpack with towels and dry socks, and a blanket.

Ciara carried the tartan rug outside and jogged over to the field to say hi to Aramis and Louie while she waited for the others to catch up. It was already getting hot; the blue sky was completely clear.

"Hey," Grandad said, walking over. "You all ready to go to the sea?"

Ciara nodded. "Are you sure you don't want to come?" she asked.

Grandad shook his head and patted Louie on the neck. "Nope, I have to go pick something up, but I'll be back before you all I expect. Did you remember your suncream?"

Ciara nodded. "Branden has it in his bag along with the towels and socks. Maddy made us pack extras just in case."

Grandad laughed. "Well, you have fun. I think you all deserve it."

"Hey, come on, let's go already," Branden said, jogging down the steps. "Woo, yeah, suns up!" He pulled his sunglasses on and smiled.

"Mum!" Maddy called. "Come on already."

"I'm coming, I'm coming," Mum said, stepping down from the porch with the picnic basket in one hand.

"Oh, here, I got it," Branden said, scooping up the basket.

They started walking down the drive towards the sea, with Mum pausing to talk to Grandad before following them. Ciara wandered along the drive enjoying the feeling of the warm sun on her arms. On really hot days in town, they had gone to the park and played in the tiny splash pool along with what had felt like every other child in the area. It had been busy and loud with people squealing as they darted in and out of the water. Even when they'd made the trip out to the seaside it had been rammed with people. Parasols and towels were put so close together there wasn't even much room for a sandcastle, but the cove near Grandad's was empty when they arrived.

"Wow," Branden said as he stepped through the edge of the dunes into the soft white sand. "How come this place isn't packed?"

Mum smiled. "It never is. Tourists sometimes come this far out, but it's rare. Most people visit the harbour and a little way up the coast from that is an old castle, it's right on the coast, and the beach there is usually much busier."

"OOH, can we visit it?" Maddy asked.

"Sure," Mum said, "I haven't been there for years, it'd be nice. Besides, that's where the school is."

"Really?" Ciara asked. "Do we get a bus or something?"

Mum laughed "Yeah, it's a long walk. But you all get the same bus, so Branden can keep an eye on you and I think I'll drive you for at least the first week."

"Oh man, you mean I have to look after these monsters," Branden said, nudging Ciara.

"Hey," She laughed and pushed him a little.

Branden laughed and grabbed hold of her bucket. "Give me that!" Ciara laughed, snatching at it and missing.

Branden whipped the bucket away. "Catch me if you can!" he said sprinting off across the sand. Ciara giggled and Maddy squealed as they pulled off their shoes and chased after him.

"No going in the water at the end of the cove," Mum called after them. "I'll spread the rug out."

Ciara ran through the sand, struggling to stay upright as the grains sunk through her toes. Maddy fell over and laughed as she rolled onto her back, flapping her arms and legs.

"Sand angel!" she shouted.

Ciara managed to catch Branden, throwing herself around his knees so they both fell into the soft sand giggling. "Ok, ok, I give in!" Branden laughed.

"Let's make a castle!" Maddy said. "Branden, Ciara help me make the biggest one ever!" Ciara smiled.

For the next hour, the three of them worked on their sandcastle. They made a huge mound of wet sand and Branden sculpted it into a vague castle shape while Ciara and Maddy used their sand moulds to add turreted towers and a gateway before they dug out a moat.

Mum occasionally looked up from her sunbathing spot on the picnic rug and said things like, "looking good". Eventually, they finished building their masterpiece and Maddy sat back with a huge grin on her face.

"It's the best one ever!" she said. "Can we take a picture so I can show Milly?"

"Sure, we can," Mum said, fishing her phone out of her bag.

"Wait!" Branden said. "Like, I'm pretty fed up with decorating, but I think we should add something." He grinned.

"Yeah!" Maddy beamed. "Like shells and things."

"Best go find some then," Mum said.

"I want to check that end of the cove!" Maddy said pointing to the sandy edge of the crescent."

"I'll take her," Branden said standing up. "You coming?" he asked Ciara.

Ciara sat in the sand for a second. As much fun as it had been building the castle, she really wanted to go see the jagged rocks at the end of the cove. They looked wild and interesting.

"Could I do the other end?" She asked looking from Branden to Mum.

"Ok," Mum said, "But you stay on the beach, no climbing the rocks, no going in the water."

"Promise," Ciara said looking over at the waves as they crashed over the rock, the white foam frothing over them.

Branden and Maddy picked up one of the buckets and headed off scouring the shore for stones, sea glass, and shells. Ciara scooped up the other bucket ready to explore and caught Mum looking at the waves. Mum smiled.

"They're somehow pretty," Ciara said.

"Yeah, they are," Mum smiled. "I used to come down here and paint, or write. Usually with Toby."

"Toby?" Ciara asked.

Mum laughed. "He was our farm dog, a collie. I always brought him here for a walk."

Ciara smiled. "Maybe you should paint them again." She suggested, Mum wrinkled her nose a little but smiled.

"Maybe I will," she said. "But not today, today I am going to lie in the sun," she said, flopping back on the blanket and pulling her hat over her eyes. "No going on the rocks."

"I know," Ciara said, standing up and heading down the beach.

She chose to walk along the firmer damp sand. It felt nicely cool under her feet, the day was so warm. Ciara had almost reached the black rocks when she spotted a little patch of multicoloured sea glass. She crouched down and sifted through the sand until she had found all the bits and put them in the bucket. She was just standing up when she spotted a ginger flash in the dunes.

Pushing a few stray hairs out of her face, Ciara looked again wondering what she had just seen. She had just taken a few steps when a little chestnut horse appeared through the dunes. Its rider guiding it over the soft sand towards the firmer part of the shore. Ciara blinked a few times and smiled.

As the horse drew closer, Ciara could see it had a white sock and a thin white stripe running down its dished face to the grey nose. Ciara waved at the girl about her age riding and she waved back heading over toward her.

"Hi," the girl said quietly.

"Hi," Ciara replied. She stepped a little closer to the horse, realising it was a gelding. "Wow, he's very handsome."

The girl smiled. "Thanks. I'm sorry, I didn't think there'd be anyone here."

Ciara looked out over the beach. "Yeah, it's quiet."

"Most of the tourists go up to the beach by the castle."

Ciara smiled. "Oh, we're not tourists, we live at the farm. Rook Cove."

The girl frowned a little. "The place with the two greys?"

Ciara nodded. "Louie and Aramis, they're my Grandad's."

"Do you ride them?" the girl asked, rubbing the chestnut's neck.

Ciara felt her face fall a little, she shook her head. "Aramis and Louie are a little big for me, besides they aren't backed yet."

"Oh," the girl's face fell a little. "I kinda hoped maybe someone had turned up who could ride with us. There aren't many people around here, even fewer who ride."

Ciara nodded. "Well, I ride, just, I don't have a pony."

"You like horses though?" the girl asked.

Ciara nodded. "My name's Ciara by the way. That's my Mum, my brother Branden and my sister Maddy."

"I'm Molly, this is Ranger." The horse scraped at the sand a little with his hoof and tossed his head. "We came down to take a walk in the sea, cool him down. There's not much shade in our field."

"Where do you live?" Ciara asked. "I think I saw you here before."

Molly nodded. "We come down most days. I live in the cottage, Holly tree. It's on the other side of the cove. I guess we're sort of neighbours."

Ciara smiled. "Do you go to school in the town by the castle?"

Molly nodded. "Are you staying then? Not just visiting?"

Ciara nodded, but she felt her smile falter a little. "Yeah, we're living with my Grandad for a bit, while my Dad is abroad for work."

"Well, it's nice to meet you. I guess we'll see you around," Molly said, she bit her lip. "Maybe, maybe sometime you could come over. It'd be nice to have someone horsey to talk to."

"I'd like that," Ciara said with a smile.

The girl rode off, walking towards the centre of the cove and letting Ranger, the chestnut, splash in the cool water. Ciara picked up her bucket and headed back towards Mum. As she walked, Ciara couldn't help but look back at Ranger and Molly, wondering what it would be like if that were her and Misty.

Mum had unpacked lunch when she got back. Branden was eating a bag of crisps while helping Maddy add shells to one of the towers. Ciara passed her the sea glass and Maddy's face lit up with excitement as she started putting the glass around the castle-like windows.

Branden was reaching for a shell when his phone buzzed. He picked it up and flicked on the screen, Ciara watched as his face fell, and he looked at her.

"What?" she asked.

"It's Olivia." He handed the phone over to Ciara so she could read the text message.

As her eyes scanned the words, Ciara felt her heart break, tears sprang up in her eyes. She stood up.

"Ciara?" Mum asked.

"Misty, Misty's gone, she's gone. Mrs. Barron sold her!" she said, her voice wavering.

She dropped the phone and started to run, thinking only about escaping everyone, everything. She heard Branden and Mum call after her but didn't stop. It never occurred to her that she had no keys to get into the house, she didn't even think about where she was running to. She struggled on through the shifting sand, her vision blurred by the tears in her eyes. Where was she? Misty? The tears streamed down her face.

Ciara reached the boarded walk that ran through the dunes and ran over it, her feet pounding on the boards as she went. The platform wound through the dunes and as Ciara ran this way and that, she stumbled but kept going, vaguely aware that Mum was behind her calling for her to stop, but she didn't.

At the road she paused to check there were no cars and then she was jogging up the drive, sniffling as she tried to stop herself crying long enough to get back. As she drew closer she could see Louie and Aramis, her first thought was to hide in the paddock with them.

Aramis especially seemed to know something was wrong as he came trotting over to the fence.

Then, there was Grandad, stood in the driveway. Ciara flew to him, her sobs becoming more frequent. He hugged her close asking her what was wrong and between heaving breaths, she tried to tell him.

"Ciara, Ciara, it's ok," Grandad said.

"No, no, it's not, she's gone Grandad, she's gone and I don't know where," she cried.

Grandad crouched down and took hold of her shoulders. He smiled at her as she tried to control her tears.

"I know," Grandad said. "It was supposed to be a surprise." Ciara looked up at him confused. He shook his head with a smile. "We never counted on your friend texting Branden."

"What?" Ciara asked.

Grandad stood up and took her hand, leading her over to the little stable block. The old coach shed was stood open for the first time, and Grandad guided her towards it. Inside Ciara realised there was a little stall and stood there, happily eating hay from a net, was

Misty. Ciara's eyes grew wide and she turned uncomprehending to Grandad. He smiled.

"Well, aren't you going to say hello?"

Ciara began to cry again and rushed into the stable, throwing her arms around Misty's neck. The little pony whickered at her and nibbled at her pockets. Ciara pulled back a little and looked over at Grandad just as Mum caught up. Seeing Ciara was ok she just smiled and hugged Grandad.

"You got back ok," Mum said.

Grandad nodded. "Going to need to sort out a proper stable for her though, this was the old goat pen."

"Stable," Ciara said. "You mean she can stay?"

"Well, she is yours," Grandad said.

"Mine?" Ciara said shocked.

Grandad chuckled. "You're ready, responsible enough I think. Mind, you need to take care of her and I expect her to help lead out the boys when they're ready."

Ciara beamed. "Thank you! Thank you!" She darted over and hugged Grandad and Mum before racing back to Misty. Her very own pony.

Chapter 10

Ciara jumped awake the next morning. Pushing the bed covers aside she stood up and pulled back the pink curtains just enough to peer out. Down below she could see Aramis and Louie's heads over their stable doors, and, next to them, the open shed door, through which she could just make out Misty. It was real. It was all real, for a moment when she had opened her eyes, Ciara had feared that Misty being here was all a dream, but she was here and she was hers. She sighed and flopped back onto the bed with a huge smile on her face.

The evening before, when Branden and Maddy had caught up to them, they had all been introduced to Misty. Maddy had been almost as excited as Ciara, she loved all animals, and having one in the family, even if it wasn't the puppy she begged for every Christmas, made her day. Branden had lent her his phone to call Olivia and, once they had stopped squealing to each other, Ciara had made her promise to come and visit at some point.

For the rest of the night, she had brushed Misty, told her everything that had happened while they were apart, and finally just sat on a hay bale watching her eat. Grandad had wandered in later, he said it was to bring her in for dinner, but Ciara thought it was more about meeting Misty properly with just her there.

He told her how he had organised everything with Mum's help. Mrs. Barron had been surprised when he had called, but once they had been chatting for a while, she seemed happy to let Misty go. He said she was glad someone loved her that much. Grandad had started chuckling when they talked about how unsuitable she had been in a riding school anyway. Ciara had smiled when Misty had snorted loudly, just at that moment.

Ciara sat up again on the bed. She grabbed her clothes, threw them on, and raced downstairs, pausing at the door to shout morning to Mum as she poked her head out of the kitchen door, a mug of coffee in one hand.

Scampering over the farmyard, Ciara paused to pat Aramis and Louie, before flinging herself into the little shed. Misty's head popped over the door and she whickered at Ciara.

"Good morning to you too," she beamed.

"Wondered how long it would be before you showed up," Grandad smiled as he appeared in the doorway with a wheelbarrow of hay. "Have you had breakfast yet?"

Ciara shook her head as she reached out to pet Misty, absently scratching her neck. The bay mare snuggled into her happily and Grandad grinned as he shook his head.

"Well, tell you what, let's put them all out for a bit, we can make sure they're happy, then we'll grab some breakfast. After that, we can sort this space out a bit. I couldn't work out how to convert it into a proper stable without spoiling the surprise." Ciara grinned. "Maybe then we can get you out for a ride."

Ciara's eyes widened. "But, I mean, what about tack?"

Grandad smiled. "Mrs. Barron agreed to sell it with her, apparently you and this pony belong together and everyone knows it," he said, reaching out and patting Misty. "We are going to have to take a trip down to Lowes though, get her a headcollar and a few bits. I think the numnah on that saddle is as old as me," he laughed.

Ciara held the gate while Grandad turned out Louie and Aramis in their little paddock before Grandad handed over the headcollar to her.

"It's too big by miles, but she'll be ok for one morning I'm sure. We'll pop her in the paddock next to the boys, they can learn about each other over the fence for a while," he said.

Ciara jogged over to Misty and slipped the headcollar on her. Even at its smallest, the noseband threatened to fall off her nose, but she followed Ciara happily across the little yard to the paddock where Grandad stood holding the gate. Ciara led her inside and slipped off the headcollar. Misty looked around herself and let out a little shout. She trotted over to the fence where Louie had appeared. They sniffed each other a little and she let out a little shriek, stamping her foot. Grandad laughed and Ciara looked at him confused.

"She's just telling him who's boss," he said with a smile. "Mind yourself, Louie."

Aramis came over to say hello next, and after a few little sniffs, they began to cautiously groom each other over the fence. Grandad put his arm around Ciara and smiled, guiding her towards the house.

"I think they'll be fine. Let's go get us some breakfast and round up the troops so we can fix her up somewhere a little nicer to sleep huh?" he said.

Ciara smiled, she glanced back over her shoulder to see Misty wander away from the fence. She nibbled at the grass a little, before dropping down and rolling in the dirt happily. She shook her head and followed Grandad inside to the smell of coffee and bacon.

As soon as they had breakfast, Grandad had everyone come out to Misty's stable. He pulled open the double doors and put his hands on his hips. After scanning the whole place he nodded his head.

"I think there's only one thing to do," he said.

"What?" Branden asked. "Knock it down?"

"Very funny," Grandad said, nudging him. "Girls, Laura, you start cleaning up a bit, Branden, you come with me to the garage. I think what we need to do is put up an extra partition piece, bring the whole stable forward a little, then we can rehang the door so that Misty has the same view as Aramis and Louie." Grandad said.

"What used to be in here?" Maddy asked, picking up some old dusty tools and stacking them in the corner.

"Oh, well," Grandad smiled. "This was where I kept the gig I drove, then when Max retired it was the temporary goat pen."

"What happened to the gig, did you sell it?" Ciara asked, going over to Maddy and helping her move some old wooden sheets.

"Oh no, I still have it," Grandad said.

"Where?" Mum asked.

"Oh man, it's not in the garage is it?" Branden asked. "I still want to play the guitar."

"Don't worry, it isn't in the garage. You remember I told you how I bought Aramis from my friend Ciara," She nodded. "Well, he owns two cottages around the bend in the cove."

"Holly tree," Ciara said quietly.

"Yeah," Grandad smiled. "How'd you know that?"

"I met a girl on the beach," Ciara said. "She said she lived there, she has a pony."

Grandad nodded his head. He picked up a screwdriver and motioned Branden to take the weight of the door while he started taking off the hinges.

"Yes, he said the renters had a horse. The other cottage, Yew Tree, it's, well it's not exactly habitable. Davey was going to do it up, before, well before he was ill, but now it's just sat empty. The family in Holly Tree keeps an eye on it and I go down once in a while, check things over, and sometimes fix things in Holly if they need doing. In exchange Davey lets me keep the old gig in the garage there. It's safe enough. Branden, got that door?" Branden nodded and Grandad pulled out the last screw. Branden and Grandad moved it to one side. "Right, let's get that panel and sort it out."

For the next few hours, Ciara found herself sweeping the floor and moving old equipment Grandad had abandoned in the shed. Mum swung between giggling and complaining that Grandad was a hoarder who didn't know what a bin was. Branden and Grandad maneuvered a wooden panel inside and set it up. Soon Misty had a proper stable, one she could look out of over the farm. They took off one of the two double barn doors and stacked it inside, putting bolts in place so they could fasten the other door closed still.

"There," Grandad said, whipping his hands on his jeans. "Looks great."

"It looks odd," Branden said. Everyone turned to look at him. "Oh, come on, we have a stone building with two stone stables with painted green doors, then a wooden stable in brown, and then another green door!"

"He's right," Grandad said. "Only thing to do is paint the wood green. I'll go get you the paint, Branden." Grandad chuckled.

"Wait! What?" Branden said. "Oh, man."

Ciara couldn't help but start laughing and soon Mum and Maddy joined in too. Branden looked at them and rolled his eyes.

"You walked right into that one," Mum said, putting her hand on his shoulder.

Grandad appeared with a tin of green paint and a brush, waving it at Branden. "There you go, you can get on with that while I take Ciara down to get Misty a headcollar."

"You owe me a Toblerone," Branden said, nudging Ciara. She just giggled.

*

Ciara stepped into the barn and stopped. Lowe's feed store was much bigger than she had imagined. In the past she had bought all of her riding things online, only ever going into one tiny tack shop Mrs. Barron knew to buy a hat. That place was crammed into a converted house, Lowes was a whole barn. The front was full of horse treats, rugs, numnahs, and other horse wear, behind that, was a huge assortment of feed and bedding, there was even an upstairs where Grandad said they had boots, coats, and riding things. Ciara's eyes drifted from one place to another not sure where to look first. Grandad ushered her inside with a smile.

"It's so big," Ciara said in awe.

"I suppose," Grandad said. "Will you be alright looking for a headcollar while I go ask about a couple of things?"

Ciara nodded, her mouth still hanging open. She drifted towards a big long rack of headcollars. There was everything from neon webbing types, to chunky leather ones with big brass buckles. Ciara tried to focus, scanning the rows of different colours. She hadn't really thought about what colour she would choose for Misty. Her eyes fell on a nice webbing one that was a mixture of purples and blues. Ciara smiled. It was perfect. She found one in Misty's size and a nice purple rope that would match.

Grandad came over and smiled at her. "Found one then?"

Ciara nodded. "You think it'll suit her."

"I do," Grandad nodded. "I got some feed sorted for her, but I think we'll need a bucket and some brushes too."

They started walking around picking out things. A purple feed bucket, some brushes, a hoof pick, and a little box to put them in. It was so much fun Ciara didn't think about what it would cost until Grandad led her over to the numnahs.

"Last thing, you definitely need a new numnah and girth," he said.

That was the moment Ciara paused, looking at the price tag on the closest girth. "I, I don't think I have enough pocket money," she said, sagging a little.

Grandad laughed. "Consider it payment for seeing to Louie and Aramis," he said. "Should we get the purple one? Might as well go for a theme."

Ciara smiled and nodded, picking up a purple numnah from the rack. Grandad had measured the girth from her old saddle and found one similar to it and picked it up, putting it in the bucket with the brushes.

"Come on," Grandad said.

He guided Ciara to the checkout near the barn door and the lady on the till rang everything through. She could barely believe it. Misty was hers and she had all these things to kit her out with, no old worn numnah.

"Oh, Ciara, go grab a tin of saddle soap, need a new one," Grandad said as they were almost finished.

Ciara darted over to a shelf they had passed earlier and picked a tin up from the shelf. As she spun around to rejoin Grandad and bumped into someone.

"Sorry," she said, looking up only to see Molly.

"Hi," she smiled.

"Hi," Ciara replied.

"Saddle soap huh, are you cleaning the big horse's tack?" she asked, looking at the tin in Ciara's hand.

Ciara shook her head. "Actually no, I got a pony."

"Really?" Molly said. "Since yesterday."

"Yeah," Ciara giggled. "It was a surprise."

"That's some surprise," Molly smiled. "What is she? He?"

"She, Misty, she's a Connemara," Ciara said.

"Ciara," Grandad called, breaking their conversation. Ciara looked over her shoulder at Grandad and then back at Molly.

"I have to go," she said.

"Sure," Molly smiled. "Maybe I'll see you at the beach?"

"Yeah," Ciara smiled. She darted back towards Grandad and slipped the saddle soap on the counter. As the lady behind the desk chatted to Grandad and he started to pay, Ciara's thoughts drifted to the idea of the beach and riding along it. Part of her was desperate to go and canter along the sand, but a small part of her was nervous too. She'd only ridden Misty outside of the school a handful of times and even then she had been with other kids, other ponies, and Mrs. Barron. Grandad put his wallet away in his pocket and smiled picking up the feed sack, while Ciara gathered the assortment of things they had gotten for Misty.

As they made their way to the car, they passed a large notice board and something caught Ciara's eye. A large notice was pinned in the centre with a picture of an old house at the top. Something about it looked familiar. Under the picture were the details of a show, a long list of events. Grandad came to stand beside her.

"Well, I never. Look at that," he said, Ciara looked up at him with a frown.

"What is it Grandad?" Ciara asked.

A smile spread over his face. "That's the old Manor house show. The one Max and I won the trophy at."

"Really?" Ciara smiled, so that was why she recognised the house on the leaflet, it had been in the pictures Grandad had shown them. "We should go, even if it's just to watch."

"Oh, well, that sounds interesting," Grandad said with a smile. "Yes, yes maybe we could go for a look down that way. The riding school I told you about is close to there anyway, I spoke to your Mum about it and we both agree it would probably be a good idea for you to still have lessons." Ciara looked at him a little worried. She didn't like the idea of ever riding anyone but Misty. "On Misty, of course," he added as if he had read her thoughts.

Ciara smiled and Grandad nudged her with his arm. "Come on, let's go try her new wardrobe on her eh, maybe you could have a little ride around the paddock too. Once she's settled in a bit I dare say you'll be off down to the beach, but I think you should stick to the paddock for a couple of days." Ciara nodded and followed him out of the shop with a bigger smile on her face than she would have thought possible a few days before.

Chapter 11

Ciara pulled the brush over Misty's back; it was nice to have her own brushes rather than borrowing an old one of Grandad's. When she had come back from Lowes, Branden had already finished painting the outside of Misty's new stable to match Aramis and Louie's. He'd even hung a bit of wood on a hook fastened to the door with the word Misty painted on it in white.

"We might need to get him two Toblerone's," Grandad had said, winking at her and making her laugh.

Misty had trotted over when Ciara had come to the gate. She looked relaxed and happy, enjoying having her own grass to eat in the sunshine. Mrs. Barron always gave her horses a few hours each day in the field and one day a week off, but this must have felt like a holiday to Misty, Ciara thought. She had put on the new headcollar they had bought and it had fitted perfectly, plus she thought the colour really suited her.

Once Misty had been tied up near the mounting block, she had fetched all the new brushes and started cleaning the dust from Misty's coat. Obviously, the mare had enjoyed a good scrub in the dirt, but it didn't take long before she was as shiny as she had been when she went into the field that morning.

Ciara fished the mane comb out of her little box and began to comb through Misty's thick dark mane. The little bay mare turned to look back over her shoulder at Ciara and she lent into Misty's mane hugging her, feeling the solidness of the pony's neck. It was like a dream. Ciara finished untangling the knots in Misty's mane and tail just as Grandad came over carrying her tack. He placed it on the mounting block with a smile.

"Well, it could do with a clean, but here it is," he smiled.

Ciara frowned. "Grandad," she bit her lip. "Could you, maybe, show me how to clean it later?"

"Something else they didn't teach you eh?" he said. Ciara smiled and nodded. "Well, I'll show you. First, though, let's see this little lady in action."

Ciara smiled. Grandad showed her how to strip the old numnah and girth off the saddle. He suggested they clean both and keep them as spares, placing both carefully on the ground beside Ciara's little grooming box. Then, with a bit of help, Ciara put the new purple numnah and girt on Misty's familiar saddle. It somehow looked much better with the new pad under it.

Grandad lifted Misty's saddle onto her and settled it in place, showing Ciara exactly where it should sit. Then he stood back while Ciara fastened up the girth. She took the bridle from Grandad and slipped it over Misty's nose, gently pulling her ears through the headpiece. She fastened the buckles and soon enough Misty was tacked up and ready to ride.

Ciara picked up her riding hat and pulled it on her head, fastening her chin strap. Grandad nodded.

"Ok, up you go," he said.

Ciara led Misty to the mounting block and began to climb up the little wooden steps. Part of her was so excited she felt like she could barely breathe, and part of her was nervous, wondering if riding Misty here would be like it was at riding school. She had waited so long for this moment. Taking a deep breath, Ciara picked up the reins, put her foot into the stirrup, and gently sprang into the saddle. Misty stood as happily as she always had and Ciara smiled, relaxing a little.

"Ok, in the paddock," Grandad said with a smile. "We'll stick to this bottom bit, it's nice and flat."

"Ok," Ciara said.

She walked Misty to the gate and Grandad let her in. She and Misty began to walk around the bottom part of the paddock and with every step, Ciara felt herself relax. Misty felt just like she always had done. After a few circles in one direction, Ciara changed direction, riding the other way. Louie and Aramis had come over to the fence line to watch and Misty swished her tail at them as they walked by making Ciara giggle.

"She looks good," Grandad called, leaning against the fence. "Shall we see a little trot?"

Ciara nodded, looked ahead and asked Misty gently to move on. She immediately started to trot around, Ciara rising and sitting to each beat. Ciara felt the paddock whizz by and smiled even more.

"Nice," Grandad said. "Now let's try walking a circle, good. Now see if you can feel her body move from side to side, underneath the saddle. Add a little energy to your inside leg as it moves inwards, in time with the swing of her barrel," Ciara concentrated and felt her leg swing inwards as Misty moved, doing as Grandad asked.

"Yes. See her inside hind leg is stepping under her body a little more there? That's the beginning of collection. When we get her to step slightly more under her body like that, the angle of her pelvis changes, and then she can round her back and lift her withers easily. Now she's carrying a little more weight on her hindquarters, and she will find it easier to carry you. It helps make her body more athletic. This way she's much less likely to develop a sore back when she is older. That's very good. Let's try the other way, trot first, then walk the circle."

Ciara and Misty trotted across the diagonal, changed direction, and trotted around together before slowing back to walk and circling around. She tried to do as Grandad had said, noticing that once again she could feel Misty's body move from side to side under the saddle, and then adding a little extra energy to her inside leg, as it was coming back into the middle.

"That's the way," Grandad said. Ciara smiled. "So, are we sticking with a walk and trot today, or do you think we should push it and go for third gear?" He patted Misty's neck and she snorted. "Well, I think we know her thoughts."

Ciara laughed. She headed out onto the little circle she had created around the bottom of the paddock and began to trot around again. After a couple of circles, she sat, thought about cantering, and felt Misty burst gently into a canter. Ciara almost closed her eyes, a smile spreading over her face as they sped around the paddock. Part of Ciara felt like she was wild and free, while the other felt as safe as if she were on a rocking horse. Misty swept around the paddock, three times before Ciara asked her to slow to a stop.

"Quite the speed on her," Grandad laughed. Ciara giggled.

She changed direction and cantered once more in the other direction, zipping past Aramis and Louie. On her second circle, Louie decided to join in, leaping up and cantering around the paddock. Ciara wondered for a second how Misty would react, but the mare stayed completely calm. Ciara asked her to slow and she did. Once they were walking, Misty tugged at the reins a little.

"Let her stretch out," Grandad said and Ciara gave Misty her head a little. She stretched out her neck and shook her mane, before looking over at Louie who was still doing acrobatic tricks by the fence.

"You're not impressing her Louie," Grandad said, chuckling.

"He's impressing me," Mum said, stepping up to the fence holding two mugs in her hand. "How's it going?"

"She's a cracking little pony," Grandad said. "With a cracking little rider if I might add."

Mum smiled. "I agree, but I still think some lessons would be a good idea."

"Well, I suppose," Grandad said. "How about we take a trip up to the riding school tomorrow? Just to look at it. I can show you the old manor."

"Really?" Ciara asked, asking Misty to stop by the fence.

"Now, what do you say we take her out for a little ride," Grandad said.

"Oh, Dad, she's only been here a day," Mum said worriedly.

Grandad nodded his head, pursing his lips a little and squinting at Misty. "She'll be fine. Laura, I know horses. She's a good pony and while she might not have been here long, Ciara's been riding her for a while. I'm not saying she should be galloping along the sand, but I don't think a walk down to the shore would hurt. I'll go with her."

Mum didn't look too sure, but she nodded anyway. Grandad opened the gate and let Ciara and Misty walk out into the yard. With Grandad beside her, they began to walk towards the driveway.

"Just a walk though, right," Mum called after them.

Ciara looked back over her shoulder with a smile to see Mum throw a hand up exasperatedly and shake her head. Ciara smiled.

Misty walked happily beside Grandad looking all around herself, she didn't seem at all alarmed or concerned, more inquisitive. Aramis and Louie followed them most of the way down the drive, right up until their paddock ended. Misty paused for a second as if wondering why the boys had stopped, but when Ciara gave her a pat and asked her to walk on, she did happily.

They reached the road and stopped looking to make sure it was clear before crossing over to the edge of the dunes. Ciara had always walked through the dunes following the old wooden planked path that ran through them, but she really wasn't sure about riding on the beams. She glanced over at Grandad.

"Do we ride on the wooden path?" she asked.

"I wouldn't," Grandad said. "I mean, I know Miss Misty isn't as heavy as Louie or Aramis, but it isn't really designed for the weight of a horse. We'll go the other way."

"Other way?" Ciara asked.

Grandad led her to one side along a little sandy path that ran parallel to the road for a while and then turned off towards the top end of the cove. Ciara realised this must have been the track that Molly and Ranger had used to get to the beach.

Soon enough they were riding through the dunes and Misty was using the opportunity to try and snatch some of the grass growing along the high dune sides as they went.

"Max used to do that," Grandad said. "It isn't a drive-through," he muttered looking at Misty. She passively looked back at him and stuck her tongue out, clinking her bit as she did. Grandad raised an eyebrow and Ciara giggled.

"She's always done that," she said.

"Mares," Grandad muttered.

The dunes began to flatten out and open up as the cove came into view. Sure enough, Ciara realised they had come out by the black rugged rocks at the top part of the cove. Misty regarded the expanse of sand and sea with a little apprehension but happily followed Grandad onto the shoreline.

They wandered through the softer sand, Misty picking her way carefully over it, to the firmer damp sand by the sea. Here, Misty stopped for a second and looked out over the sea, Ciara did too. There was something almost magical about the gentle rhythmic waves lapping on the shore. After a few moments of watching the shimmering sun on the water, they headed closer. Grandad walked alongside as they stepped right up to the frothing waves.

Ciara had half expected the sea to worry Misty. The riding school had been close to town, well inland. She wasn't sure Misty had even been to a beach, but either sometime in the past she had, or she was braver than Ciara thought most horses were. Without flickering, the little bay mare put her hoof into the water and happily walked along as the sea lapped around her hooves. Grandad grinned.

"A proper seahorse," he chuckled.

They walked together all along the length of the cove, Grandad giving her pointers and commenting on how Misty was doing. Ciara tried to listen to him, but all she could think about was the feel of Misty as they walked along. It wasn't too long before they reached the far side of the cove. They stopped again and Grandad looked from the ocean to Misty and back. He nodded his head slowly.

"Do you think you two can walk back along the cove together?" Grandad asked. "It's a lot easier on my old legs to walk along the plank walk," he chuckled.

Ciara looked back along the cove and nodded his head. "Yeah, we'll be fine."

"Right, I'll watch you down the beach and then meet you by the road crossing, ok?" Grandad said.

Ciara nodded. "Ok."

Ciara turned Misty around and headed back down the beach toward the black rocks. When Grandad had been with them, Ciara had found herself distracted, trying to both enjoy the sights around her and the feeling of riding Misty somewhere other than the school, while still trying to listen to what Grandad was saying. Now though it was just them.

There was no other sound but the breaking waves. A slight sea breeze tugged at Ciara's hair and the spray of the ocean splashed at her legs. It was so wild and yet so calming, Ciara wandered along, letting Misty decide how close to the sea they should be. It was amazing. She was here with Misty.

"Can you believe it?" she said to Misty. "I thought this was going to be the worst time in my life." She looked at the sparkling water. "Now though," she smiled as she patted Misty's neck. "Now, it might be the best."

It was true. The farm had so much room, a garden, horses, and sheep, not to mention Grandad. The beach was a few minutes' walk away and so quiet, and peaceful. Now Misty was here and she was all Ciara's. The only thing missing was Dad. Ciara felt sad for a second, but Misty tugged at the reins a little, breaking Ciara from her thoughts.

They were nearly at the outcrop of rock now and reluctantly Ciara turned Misty away from the shore back towards the dunes and home. She smiled as they wandered together over the softer sand, soon enough she'd be able to come here and canter along the sand like Molly did. Perhaps they could even meet up with Molly and

Ranger and ride together. She wondered where else they could ride too. Grandad hadn't mentioned any other rides, but there seemed to be no end of fields around the farm, perhaps there were other hacks to discover. Ciara smiled as they wandered through the dunes, imagining what it would be like to go exploring with Misty.

Grandad was waiting for them by the edge of the road, sitting on the fence. Misty stopped beside him and rubbed her nose on a bit of the fence. Grandad patted her neck.

"Have fun?" he asked. Ciara nodded. "Good, because I think Miss Misty here might be the perfect person to give Master Louie a confidence boost when we come down to the beach for a walk. Who knows, maybe she can even escort Aramis down here when I back him."

"I think we'd like that." Ciara smiled.

Grandad nodded and pushed himself up off the fence. "Come on then, let's get home, get us some supper and this little lady some too." Misty snorted and Ciara laughed, patting her neck.

Chapter 12

Ciara lent on the fence as Grandad worked Aramis around the paddock. The big grey gelding moved fluidly and happily, ignoring both Misty stood beside Ciara munching on some hay in a net hung on the fence and Louie who was staring at him from their paddock. Today was the day Grandad said. He was going to get on Aramis again. Ciara hadn't really seen Aramis in full tack, but when Grandad had brought out his saddle and bridle, the big horse had looked rather keen.

Misty snorted and rubbed her head on Ciara. She didn't seem to realise what the big deal was and it made Ciara smile. Grandad stopped Aramis and took off the long lines. He nodded at Ciara and she quietly opened the gate and lifted the little wooden mounting block inside the paddock.

"Ready?" she said. Grandad smiled; he looked a lot less nervous than Ciara felt.

"Yes, he'll be fine. Aramis has had someone sit on him before you know, it was just a while ago. See, we move slowly, we need to make sure he's physically capable of what we're asking him to do, but also mentally ready. I only start riding my horses when they are four, sometimes five. Their bodies aren't developed enough before that. " Louie snorted and started tossing his head. Grandad narrowed his eyes at him. "Of course, there are always exceptions when a horse doesn't ever mentally mature." He chuckled and Louie flicked his ears back and forth making Ciara smile.

"So, if he's already been sat on, what's next?" Ciara asked.

"Well, the first time I ever got on I just sat there a few minutes and then got off. Next couple of times I got on and rode a few paces and then stopped. Today we're going to ask him to walk a couple of big circles in each direction. Then, slowly, we'll build on that," Grandad said.

He led Aramis over to the mounting block. Aramis lined up and stood happily as Grandad climbed up the steps. He rubbed Aramis's neck, fussing over him a little.

"It's important that he doesn't walk off, or get used to moving straight away. By asking him to wait and fussing him, he doesn't get used to it being jump on and go," Grandad explained. He put his foot into the stirrup and lightly hopped up onto Aramis. As soon as he was seated, Grandad started to pat and fuss him again. He gathered up the reins but still sat for a few more seconds. Then with a gentle nudge of his legs, he said "Walk on."

Aramis began to walk off away from the mounting block. He walked around the edge of the paddock and Ciara smiled. The big grey's ears swivelled around, but on the whole, he looked very relaxed. After a couple of circles around one way, he changed direction. Finally, Grandad asked Aramis to stop, and looked over the fence at Ciara.

"You ready?" Ciara nodded. She took hold of Misty and led her into the paddock too. Grandad had suggested they give Aramis a little lesson on how to work with other horses and ponies there.

"Ok, you walk Misty around and we'll follow you, then I'll ask Aramis to turn away from her. As long as he does it, we leave his training for the day. Always end on a positive note," Grandad said. He lined Aramis up behind Misty and they set off, the big grey playing follow my leader with the little bay mare. Misty was oblivious to the strangeness of this, for her it was just like being in one of the riding school lessons, but for Aramis, it was the most exciting thing ever. He seemed to love following Misty's little black tail around the school and resisted a little when Grandad asked him to turn away, but he did do it and Grandad gave him a fuss. They changed direction and did the same thing, once again Aramis happily followed and reluctantly parted ways with Misty.

Grandad halted Aramis and hopped down from him, patting his neck. "Brilliant," he smiled. "This is going to be great. I think Aramis will follow Misty quite nicely down to the beach, she can be his security blanket," he chuckled. So did Ciara, the idea of the little pony being braver than the huge grey horse somehow seemed comical.

Grandad began to lead Aramis out of the paddock so Ciara could turn Misty loose. He had promised to take her down to the riding school in the afternoon so she could see what it was like before taking Misty down for a lesson. Ciara was feeling quite excited about it. Wouldn't it be nice, she thought, to have a lesson on her own pony? The thought made a smile cross her face while she slipped the headcollar off Misty.

*

The little riding school Grandad pulled up to was about the same size as Mrs. Barron's, but had two schools rather than one. Ciara stepped out of the car and looked around herself. There was a large field close to the car park that had been made into two paddocks. The stable yard was laid out in a U shape with black and white painted stables. A large school ran behind one side of the stables and out along the edge of the car park. The smaller arena was on the other side of the stables and was about half the side.

A girl on a grey mare was trotting around the smaller school, popping over a little cross pole. Grandad stepped up beside Ciara and put his arm around her shoulders. He nodded his head towards the yard and they walked over together. A lady with a long dark ponytail popped her head out of one of the stable doors and smiled as they approached. She stepped out and opened a big gate letting them into the little yard.

"Patrick?" she asked Grandad, and he nodded. "And Ciara right?" Ciara smiled and nodded. "I'm Sandra, Sandra Bell, welcome to Briary. I hear you might want to pop down for some lessons?"

"Yeah," Ciara said, not sure what to say.

"And you have your own pony, but she's new?" Sandra asked.

"Sort of," Ciara frowned. "I've ridden Misty for ages, but at riding school."

"We bought her from Ciara's old riding stables," Grandad said. "Just a few days ago. She's a nice pony and Ciara's good on her, but they still need direction."

Sandra smiled. "Well, I think we can do that. I'd normally have new students pop on one of my horses to see how they ride, but I hear your Grandad knows what he's doing, so maybe you could tell me which level she's at."

Grandad chuckled. "You've been talking to Dot haven't you?"

"Mrs. Fitz, yes," Sandra smiled.

"Well, I'd say she's a very decent novice," Grandad said.

"Ok, how does Saturday at 10.am sound?" Sandra asked.

"Good to me," Grandad smiled. "Do you hire out either arena?"

"I do," Sandra said.

Grandad nodded slowly and Ciara frowned. "Oh, I'm just thinking it might be a good learning opportunity for Aramis, I could bring him down sometimes while you have a lesson."

"What about Louie?" Ciara asked worried that the big grey would fret alone.

Grandad smiled. "Eh, Louie's fine, don't let him fool you. If he has food and it isn't for more than a few hours, he's absolutely fine."

"Well," Sandra said, "would you like a tour?"

Ciara smiled. They had seen almost all the stables when Ciara noticed an older lady dressed in tweed, walk in through the big gate, a spaniel running around her feet. Grandad smiled when he saw her and waved. The old lady waved back and headed towards them. As she drew closer, Ciara realised she recognised her, she was the lady from the photo, the one who had given Grandad the trophy he had won with Max.

"Morning Dot," Grandad said cheerfully.

"Morning Patrick," the lady replied with a smile. "Who have we here?" she asked, glancing in Ciara's direction. Ciara smiled a little shyly.

"This is Ciara, my eldest granddaughter. Laura and the children are staying with me while their Dad is working abroad. Ciara just got her first pony, we're sorting her out some lessons."

"Oh, a first pony," Mrs. Fitz smiled. "What sort?"

"A bay Connemara, her name is Misty," Ciara said with a smile.

"Really? A Connemara. I have a Connie up at the manor. Ozzie belongs to the girl whose parents run the holiday lets B&B. You'll have to pop up and meet her, bring Misty for a ride." Mrs. Fitz said. Ciara glanced at Grandad and smiled.

"We were planning on coming up to the show actually," Grandad said.

"Entering?" Mrs. Fitz asked with a smile.

"Oh, I don't know about that Dot," Grandad chuckled. "Maybe Ciara and Misty might, but my lads are barely backed."

"We're doing an in-hand class this year too," Mrs. Fitz said pointedly. Grandad laughed, but Ciara caught a look in his eyes that she hadn't seen before. Maybe, she thought, just maybe, they would be less spectators and more participants in the show.

*

Ciara did the girth up on Misty's saddle and clicked the buckle in place on her hat. After they had come home from the riding school, she had begged to ride out down to the beach again and Mum had finally agreed, so long as someone went with her over the road. In the end, Branden had volunteered in exchange for her help in clearing the garage at the weekend so he could play the guitar. He'd been chatting to Luke from the hardware store and they had agreed to meet up in a few weekends with a few of Luke's friends for a jam session, Branden was desperate to practice beforehand.

Misty followed Ciara over to the mounting block and she climbed the steps. Remembering what Grandad had done with Aramis earlier, she petted Misty a little before hopping on board, she then stood for a few moments fussing her again before she asked her to walk on. Branden was waiting by Misty's stable, leaning against the door.

"Ready?" he asked. Ciara smiled and nodded. "Ok, let's go."

They chatted a little as they wandered down the driveway, Branden talking about music and playing the guitar, Ciara telling him about the riding school and the show. Surprisingly Branden had been interested in the idea of the show, but mostly because he said there wasn't much going on.

They reached the road and crossed it carefully. "You want me to walk with you to the beach?" Branden asked.

Ciara thought about it for a moment. She hadn't been alone with Misty on a ride before, on one hand, the thought made her a little nervous, on the other, very excited.

"We'll go on our own," she decided to be brave.

"Ok," Branden said. "I'll wait here." He sat down on the edge of one of the dunes and pulled out his phone, flicking through some music.

Ciara smiled and urged Misty along the path they had followed the day before. They wound their way through the sand dunes and out onto the beach. Ciara asked Misty to slow down for a second. It was later in the afternoon than it had been on their first trip down to the cove. The lower sun shimmered on the dark waves making it sparkle as if it had been covered in diamonds. Ciara smiled and took a deep breath of the clean sea air.

They walked over the soft white sand down to the firmer part of the shore. Ciara decided then and there that they should trot along the sea edge. Misty was more than happy to oblige trotting along, her ears pricked. Ciara began to feel more and more confident as they went. She found it easy enough to bring Misty back to walk and she didn't even jog as they walked along to the end of the cove.

Turning around, they started to trot again. The tide had come in just enough so that they were now trotting through the sea spray. Without even thinking about it Ciara sat a few beats, thinking about cantering through the lapping waves, and then they were. Steadily cantering evenly along the sands, Misty's head held high, her ears pricked. Ciara smiled, feeling the sensations of Misty's feet pounding on the sand, the breeze in her hair, and the spray of the sea on her legs and arms.

They slowed down a way before the black rocks and stopped watching the sea. Ciara sighed. Life at Grandad's seemed blissful now somehow, Misty, cantering along Coral Cove. There was the shout of a horse from behind them and they turned to see Molly and Ranger emerge from the dunes. All they needed was a few friends, Ciara smiled and urged Misty over toward the chestnut gelding. Life was looking up. And Ciara knew her next adventure was on the way.

You did it...

Congratulations! You finished this book.

Loved this book? Consider leaving a review! Book reviews are a valuable way for you to help me share this book about Ciara and Misty with the world. If you enjoyed this book, I would love it if you could leave a review online. Ciara & Misty say a big thank you too!

Enjoy book 2 in the Coral Cove series at

www.writtenbyelaine.com

THE
CONNEMARA
ADVENTURE SERIES
FOR KIDS 8+

THE CORAL COVE SERIES

www.writtenbyelaine.com

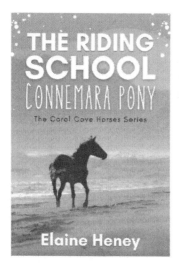

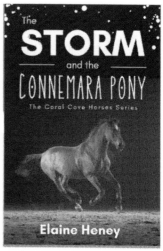

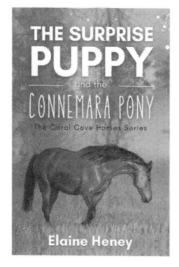

HORSE BOOKS

by #1 best-selling author
ELAINE HENEY

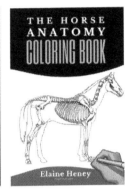

www.elaineheneybooks.com

Horse Training Resources

Discover our series of world-renowned online groundwork, riding, training programs and mobile apps. Visit Grey Pony Films & learn more: www.greyponyfilms.com Find all Elaine's books at www.writtenbyelaine.com

Made in United States
Troutdale, OR
11/28/2024

25409079R00093